Becky,

Enjoy the
Apocalypse!
Thanks for Coffin'
Hopping ☺

Julianne
Snow

GLIMPSES
OF THE
UNDEAD

A Short Story Collection

JULIANNE SNOW

Sirens Call Publications

Glimpses of the Undead

GLIMPSES OF THE UNDEAD

JULIANNE SNOW

Sirens Call Publications

THE TREEHOUSE

It walked with a sickening limp. The accompanying noise was akin to the grinding of teeth, only louder. Much louder. It was a sound that reverberated inside your head, warning you of its imminent appearance.

A voice snaked out of the darkness at me. "It's comin' this way!"

It was Billy. Stupid Billy.

"Shhhh! It's gonna hear you!"

The response was barely above a whisper. Too quiet for poor Billy to hear and likely too intelligent for him to understand.

The grinding noise seemed to get closer. Out of the corner of my eye I could see it. Everything about it was frightening. The slack, waxen face. The left eye drooping out of the socket and laying half eaten on the discoloured flesh of its cheek. The gore pocked clothing relaying the message that it had eaten - recently. The worst sight was its left leg; the skin had been flayed off of most of the lower half and one of the bones was broken. The sound that we were hearing was the scraping of the ends together as it limped awkwardly in our direction.

We didn't have the best hiding spot but sometimes you have to make do with what is around when you're on the move. Technically we were just on the opposite side of a large planked fence, but the fence was broken. It looked like a herd of elephants came through a section just a few feet down from us, but we knew what really happened.

We saw it all go down. About three days ago, a group of survivors were fleeing an onslaught of Zombies on the road. With the corpses so thick in front of them, they changed directions and drove straight through the fence.

In any other situation, the action would have been cool to watch but the fence was the only thing keeping the Zombies out of the yard and away from the tree that supported our sanctuary.

As we watched from our vantage point, high above the verdant ground, we saw the truck come through one length only to lose the speed needed to go completely through the length on the opposite side. Instead, it got hung up on the broken fence beneath it and stopped short.

The driver panicked and in their haste to free the floundering truck, managed only to hopelessly tangle it among the hewn boards.

Panic is a funny thing; it can give you superhero capabilities or it can paralyze you. Like a sick game of Russian roulette, it chose paralysis this time.

We listened in horror as the Zombies flooded the backyard and surrounded the car, our minds making movies of what was occurring below us. Each whisper soft sound of their decaying limbs brushing the shiny blue exterior of the truck. The dull pounding of their grimy hands on the glass, almost rhythmic in its intensity. The sharp cracking of the glass as it spider-webbed out from the point of impact. Screams assaulted our ears as the Zombies pulled the occupants through their access point. Not daring to look down lest we give away our position, we were forced to watch the translation of those sounds behind clamped eyelids.

It didn't take long but the memories of what we heard reverberate in our minds even now. Everything that we've seen and heard have melded together to produce the most horrific montages that play across the black expanse each time we close our eyes.

We knew we had to leave our makeshift home. With the hole in the fence, the backyard became a draw for them. We've waited until this moment to climb carefully down the lowered rope ladder, hoping not to attract attention to ourselves. I was the last to descend, cautiously feeling for each woven rung as I watched the scarred and lonely landscape around me, hoping I wouldn't attract any attention.

Over my left shoulder I saw it. The solitary corpse had spotted me and was now limping in our general direction. It was slow but it moved with purpose. Our only hope was to confuse it by waiting until it was in the enclosed backyard before sneaking out behind it.

Fate wanted to play a different game with us today. Not only had it stacked the deck against us with Zombies, it had also given us Billy.

Stupid Billy.

As the broken leg of the Zombie came into view around the smashed edge of the planked span of fence, Billy screamed. High pitched and girly.

He froze, his mouth forming a perfect, round hole as the scream choked in his throat. A face appeared around the damaged edge, almost comical in its surprise and hunger. Its eye locked on Billy, the milky cornea searching for something; recognition perhaps.

With another scream, matched by a strident noise of victory from the Zombie, the dance of death resumed.

The rest of us took the moment of inattention to scale back up the rope ladder, knowing that at some point, we would need to escape. The time will come; we just need to be patient.

KAMIKAZE

"Babe! You're not listening again." Melinda gently spoke into the face of her irate boyfriend. "I need to do this – it's the only way."

"There has to be another way, Mel. What you're planning is illegal and could very well get you killed! My life is not worth that." Lucas shouted back at her, hoping that his volume would help her to see sense.

"It's worth it to me," she spoke in a whisper, wiping away the tears as they coursed down her face. "We're barely making ends meet now as it is and with you not working, we'll never come up with the money for the surgery. Please understand I'm doing this for you, for us!"

Her passionate speech didn't have the desired effect on Lucas and she was disheartened to see him stalk across their modest sized, one bedroom apartment to grab his coat. "If you do this, we're over. Simple as that."

The anger was gone from his posture, but the words were sharpened like knives; each one of them penetrated her heart, causing it to burst with pain. He looked at her one last time before roughly grabbing the doorknob and jerking it toward him.

"You can't leave now, it's almost time for your medicat--"

The hard slam of the door was her only response.

***

"Is this a joke, Ma'am?" The teller asked her the question as she held the note in her left hand, a quizzical smile plastered on her face.

"I'm dead serious Miss. Put all of your money in the bag and don't try anything stupid. Got it?" To emphasize her point, Melinda opened the flap of her second hand bomber jacket so the teller could see the bomb's wiring and mechanism. "One wrong move and I will detonate myself."

With eyes now as wide as saucers, the young woman, whose nametag read 'Olive' started to transfer the money from her drawer into the canvas shoulder bag Melinda had provided. She looked neither left nor right and worked with an efficiency that startled Melinda. Has she done this before?

Melinda stared at the teller, noting her bottle blonde hair and the fake eyelashes. In fact, she was staring so intently at her she failed to notice the looks from the other bank employees. There was a sense in the air that something was going down, but by that point Melinda was too focussed on her immediate environment to notice.

That was when the bell sounded. It was loud and incessant and it almost made her lose control of her bladder. Ducking, she turned to stare at the ceiling, concerned that something bad was actually happening. Not seeing the telltale signs of smoke rising, she was unprepared for the hard body that slammed into her.

As she was knocked to the ground, Melinda's mind immediately turned its attention to the area around her. Was something close to her on fire? She still hadn't connected the alarm to the bomb strapped to her chest.

"Don't move!"

"Get off me, please! Is there a fire? We need to get out!"

"Stop moving!"

Immediately Melinda stopped struggling, the realization that the alarm had something to do with her and the robbery finally dawning on her. Trying to think fast with a knee pressed firmly between her shoulder blades, her mind drew a blank. Until she felt the mechanism of the bomb pressed firmly into her breasts.

"Get off of me or I'll blow you up too!" She waited a moment for the words to sink in before speaking again. "I have two bricks of C4 strapped to my chest and you're really not doing either of us any favours by grinding it into the ground. We're lucky it hasn't gone off yet!"

With some reluctance, Melinda could feel the body release her and was glad that she could breathe easily again. Clamouring up from the cold linoleum floor, she turned to find herself alone, the other patrons having moved as far away from her as they could. The only person in close proximity was a young man in a security uniform, his breathing laboured. She couldn't quite tell if he was breathing hard from the exertion or the possibility that he might have been blown up when he tackled her. To be honest, she didn't even care.

Taking a moment to catch her breath, she turned back to the teller's counter and reached over for the bag of money that had been forgotten in the commotion. Lifting it, she could feel the weight of the bills and it brought a smile to her face. Lucas would be able to have his operation and everything would be okay.

"I'll be leaving now. Thank you Olive." With a quick nod in the young woman's direction, Melinda strode to the double glass doors that led to the street. Pushing on the handle, she felt an unfamiliar resistance. Thinking that perhaps they only unlocked one of the doors, she positioned herself in front of the other door and pushed.

Nothing.

Turning back in confusion she searched for the guard who had taken a seat off to the side, his head between his knees. "Hey, do you have keys for this door? If you do, I suggest you let me out now."

"The doors lock automatically once the alarm is triggered." It was Olive who gave her the information.

"Well I suggest that somebody fucking unlock them before I really get angry!" Melinda fought to keep the fear from her voice. It had already taken root in her brain; what if she wasn't able to leave? What if she got caught? Would Lucas still live?

"None of us have keys to unlock them. Only the manager and her assistant do and both of them are out to lunch at the moment. Oh and the police have a master as well." It was Olive again. "Look the police will be here any minute, so-"

"Police? Who the fuck called the police?" Now Melinda was angry and terrified. Her plan was starting to fall apart and there seemed to be nothing she could do to salvage it. Lucas was going to die and there was nothing she could do about it.

As she stared out the glass paned doors, she wondered if she could simply break them and escape. It was worth a shot after all. Looking to her left, Melinda spotted a metal garbage container.

Hefting the silver canister in her arms, she rushed back to the door only to see the flashing lights of the police cruisers descending on the bank's entrance. It was too late.

Melinda dropped the garbage pail and turned toward the back of the bank. Noting the offices, she said loudly, "Okay everyone, into the back offices. Let's go! Quickly. I have a bomb strapped to me and I'm not afraid to take you all out with me."

The truth of the matter was that Melinda had no intentions of detonating the bomb. Heck, it wasn't even a real bomb. The wiring and mechanisms were real, but there was no way that she could have gotten her hands on real C4 explosives. The bomb was merely a ruse designed to scare the teller into giving her the money she desperately needed. Not that any of them knew that and she certainly wasn't going to share the information now.

Looking back toward the double doors, she could just make out the faces of the officers trying figure out what was going on in the bank. She opened her jacket to give them time to see the bomb before joining her hostages out of the direct line of sight.

"Okay, time for us to get serious here. It appears that we're stuck with each other for a while and we'd better make the best of it. Those of you that have cell phones or any electronics on you should place them all on the tables in front of you." Sometimes Melinda could really think on her feet and for some reason the instructions poured out of her mouth without much thought. It must have been from the police procedurals she watched on television all the time.

She watched intently as the patrons surrendered their phones and tablet computers to the table, trying to tell if any of them were holding back an item. The fear of the bomb on her person must have been weighing on each of them as it really didn't seem like anyone was withholding anything. "Thank you. Olive, would you be a dear and collect all of the devices in this garbage can for me?"

Melinda watched as Olive came forward to do as she was asked, her hands moving efficiently in her task. Was there nothing that flustered this young lady? Her hands weren't even shaking and they hadn't been when she loaded the money into the bag Melinda now wore across her body.

"Okay, now time for the purses." Melinda quickly ducked into the next room and picked up another garbage can, "Can you please put all of your purses in here." She spoke with a kind voice, her vain attempt at keeping her own growing panic at bay. It would serve no purpose if she lost it now.

After she had collected all of the articles that she thought to collect, she pulled out one of the chairs from the table and sat down for a moment. Her eyes never left the group as she pondered what her next step was going to be. There certainly would be no easy escape now and try as she might, she couldn't figure out a way to get the money to Lucas. Her plan had gone seriously awry and now she had hostages to think about. Hostages and a prison sentence.

***

Outside the bank, Detective Phillips was studying the schematics of the building, trying to figure out if he should have his officers storm it. He had seen the woman open her jacket inside the bank and noted the bomb, but knew that if they could get her in a blitz attack it would be over in moments. Having been a cop for so many years, there wasn't much that he missed and while the bomb looked impressive at first glance, there was something off about it. Setting his subconscious mind to work, he looked up at one of the techs to ask, "Do we have a line in there yet?"

"Just a moment, Sir. Still waiting on the phone company to patch us in." The tech was young, as so many of them were; just barely out of the police college. He stood there, waiting. There was nothing else he could do until he established who she was and what she wanted.

***

The phone on the wall next to Melinda rang with a surprising urgency, startling her. Staring at it blankly for a moment, she picked up the receiver and held it to her ear, her eyes returning to watch the small group in front of her.

"Hello. My name is Mortimer Phillips and I am a detective with the Philadelphia Police Department. May I ask whom I am speaking with?"

"Melinda Franklin." The smooth voice caught her off guard and she answered before she thought better of it. "Shit!"

"Pardon, Melinda?" She could hear the amusement in his voice and struggled to regain her composure. "Melinda, is there anything that you need in there? Can you tell me if all of the hostages are okay?"

"Yes, they're fine. And no, we don't need anything." Melinda hung the phone up after speaking, feeling a wave of guilt at not saying goodbye. She knew it was odd, but sometimes manners were hard to forget. Standing up, Melinda fought hard to think. Her emotions were starting to get the better of her. She was not a criminal and the situation she now found herself in was completely unnerving.

***

Outside in the command centre, the techs were now assembling a complete dossier on Melinda Franklin. Detective Phillips couldn't help but think he was dealing with an amateur and the thought scared him. Seasoned criminals tended to do things in a specific pattern, but the newbies were always unpredictable. He was going to have to anticipate her every move while trying to stay one step ahead of her. It was going to require a lot of juggling and skill, but he knew he was up to the task. He'd get those hostages out alive.

"Sir, here's something interesting. She has a boyfriend named Lucas Taggert and it appears that he's ill. From the insurance reports, he was turned down for an operation that could save his life and their financials paint a very dismal picture. There's no way they could have afforded it on their own."

Rubbing the stubble on his angular jaw, Phillips understood the motivation for the crime. His ex-wife had needed surgery a few years before he joined the force and without a penny to their name, they had struggled to pay for it. In the end, the strain was what had torn them apart. Jerking back from his reverie, he picked up the phone again.

***

"Why does this guy keep calling?" Melinda said under her breath to no one other than herself. The second time the phone rang was even more unnerving than the first. Not wanting to pick it up, she let it ring.

It continued to ring for long minutes, until at last, she picked it up. Placing the receiver to her ear, she waited for him to speak.

"Tell me about Lucas."

Silence was the only sound that passed along the line. Phillips had rendered her speechless. It was a long while before he spoke again.

"I understand Melinda. I get it. I was once in a position like you, but this is no way to solve it."

"You're just saying that because it's what you're supposed to say. You don't know anything about my life or understand even one tiny bit what I'm going through." Her anger made the connection electric, but Phillips was prepared for it.

"I do understand. More than you know." He was trying to connect via their shared stress and pain, and hoped his next statement would gain a little of her trust. "If you like, I can tell you about Claire."

"Who's Claire?"

"My wife. She died a few years ago." Small lies wouldn't hurt. As long as he stayed close enough to the truth for the emotion of the experience to bleed into the conversation, it would be okay. "She once needed surgery, just like Lucas does."

"I don't know what you think you know, but I don't want to talk about Lucas." For the first time, her sadness entered her voice. She hadn't been able to let Lucas see her sad, always choosing to be upbeat for him. The strain of the constant worry and the perpetual happiness had run its course and as Phillips started to talk, Melinda began to cry.

"Claire and I had only just graduated from college when she was diagnosed with cancer. Her doctors said that she would need a number of surgeries to prolong her life, but at the time, neither one of us had jobs. We'd only just graduated and opportunities in those days were shittier than they are now. Needless to say, we had to come up with the money. Claire was an orphan so she had no one to turn to and my family was poorer than dirt, so we knew we had no options there either. We spent many long nights awake, trying to think of ways to raise the money. Heck, I'm not ashamed to say that we even thought about robbing a bank too. In the end, I worked three jobs and we lived off of canned beans for 3 years before we had saved enough money to afford even one of the operations that she needed. It was hard, but we managed-"

"How did your wife die?"

The question came out of left field at him. He hadn't anticipated that she would quiz him about his experience. "Car crash."

"I'm sorry to hear that she died that way. Perhaps it saved her from a life of pain and suffering." The hardness in her voice startled him. At some point during his story, she had regained her composure. He was going to have to work harder to connect with her.

"Perhaps. But that's not-"

"You sound very cold when you talk about her. Why is that?"

It was at that moment one of the techs handed him a piece of paper. Reading it over quickly, Phillips realized he'd made an error; Melinda Franklin worked as a therapist

17

at a drug rehabilitation centre. She was certainly not going to be an easy nut to crack…

***

Melinda knew the silence on his end was telling. Either she had stopped him in his tracks, or she had upset him. Either way, it was the break she needed to end the call. "When you have an answer for me, give me a call back."

Exhaling loudly and running her hands through her hair, Melinda was so glad the conversation was over for the time being. While she felt deeply sorry the detective had gone through such turmoil, it wouldn't help her to get too close to him. Keeping her distance is what she needed, especially if she was going to figure out how to get out of the bank alive.

"Olive, is there a back door to this place?"

"Ummm, yeah," she answered. "But they'll likely be watching that one too."

While Olive was unaware she had probably just saved Melinda's life, Melinda wasn't. "Good point, thanks!"

Looking around the room, Melinda studied the scared faces of the hostages. There were 11 of them in total; far fewer than she would have thought would be in the bank that Tuesday afternoon. Chalking up the head count to the marvels of internet banking, she turned her attention to the television set that adorned one of the walls. "Does that thing actually hook up to an antenna or anything?"

"Yeah. We use it to watch television on our lunch breaks when we can." This time the answer came from an older woman who also worked at the bank. Her nametag said Rose.

"Thank you Rose. Would you mind turning it on for me? I'd like to see what the news is saying about all of this."

Rose stood and went to the television, turning it on by pressing a button on the side. She picked up the remote and tuned to one of the local news stations. The broadcast that greeted them was not what any of them expected,

***

"Melinda, where the fuck are you?" Lucas spoke into his cell phone as he left a message for his girlfriend. "Have you seen the news yet? I just want to know if you're safe. Call me back the second that you get this!"

His phone rang the moment that he disconnected the call and Lucas hurried to answer it. "Melinda?"

"No, I'm sorry. This is Detective Mortimer Phillips-"

"Holy shit! Is Melinda alright? Is she hurt? Don't tell me she's dead, I don't think I can handle hearing that over the phone!" The words came out in a rush, his panic evident by the barrage of questions he fired at the officer.

"Is this Lucas Taggert?" The smooth voice was patient and reassuring, even during a question.

"Yes, it is. May I ask why you're calling me?"

"Lucas, are you aware that your girlfriend is holding hostages at the First National Bank in Philadelphia?" He asked the question first, hoping the surprise would elicit information that he didn't already have.

"She's what? Hostages? Are you fucking with me?" His voice reeked of incredulity and confusion; Phillips believed he knew nothing of the hostages at least. "I've been trying all afternoon to get hold of her since the attacks started."

"What attacks?" Now it was Phillips turn to be confused.

"C'mon man! You're the police – you know exactly what's going on. The reports of the attacks have been all over the news this afternoon." Lucas paused to take a breath and glance at the incoming call on his screen, "Hang on a sec, will ya? It's Melinda – finally!"

He was gone before Phillips even had a second to answer.

***

"Lucas?"

"Where the fuck have you been Melinda? I've been trying to get hold of you all afternoon. Are you okay?" He stopped there, giving her time to answer him.

"Listen, Lucas. I'm in Philly, at the bank-"

"What the fuck? Are you telling me that cop is right? Do you seriously have hostages?"

"Cop?"

"Yeah some guy's waiting on the other line; says he's a cop. Told me you were at a bank in Philadelphia with hostages. Please tell me you didn't..." His voice trailed off in frustration.

"Yes, I'm at the bank in Philly and yes, I do have hostages, but it's not what you think. I didn't take hostages; I sort of got forced into it-"

"Forced into it? What did they do? Hold a gun to your head and make you take them hostage? C'mon Mel, let's be serious here."

"I am trying to be serious Lucas. What does the cop want?"

"I don't know; you called before he could tell me." Lucas stopped for a moment, his eyes drifting back to the muted television set in the apartment. "You need to get out of there, Mel. They're almost where you are."

"I know Lucas, but I can't get out. I've got a street full of police out front and..." Melinda's voice trailed off, not wanting to say the words aloud. "Take your bug-out bag and leave the city. Go to our rally point and if I can meet you, I will."

"I'm not leaving without you Mel. No way."

"I love you too, but you have to. Pretty soon, there will be too many of them. Go now. Got it?" Melinda choked up as she spoke, not wanting to be left behind but knowing that he had to leave her. Not wanting to hear him argue with her anymore, she disconnected the call.

***

"Lucas?" It was the cop again. Once Melinda hung up, it brought him right back to his initial call. "Was that Melinda?"

"Look man, you've got bigger problems than Melinda... They'll kill you and then turn you. Get out of the city while you still can!"

Phillips was left with the high-pitched tone of an available line in his ear and the confused thoughts of a man who didn't know what to make of the conversation he'd just had. What the hell was going on?

***

Lucas grabbed his bug-out bag and slung it over his shoulders. He then turned and picked up Melinda's, putting it on backward, similar to the way a mother carried her baby. Despite her instructions to leave the city, he knew that she would need his help getting out. He left their small apartment, glancing back to the muted television, hoping that the throngs of the undead were no longer on the screen. With a heavy sigh, he closed the door on their old life and left to save the woman that he loved.

***

The atmosphere in the bank was tense as all eyes were riveted to the television's screen. No one said much of anything, all of them staring at the carnage coming their way.

"Holy shit! Is that Jefferson and Wilfred? That's only two blocks from here..." It was Olive who put voice to what they were all seeing. Zombies were advancing and there was nothing that any of them could do.

"If you guys want to call your loved ones, I'm totally fine with that." Melinda set the garbage bag down on the table after taking it out of the can, opening the bag wide so that everyone could see their phones. "I just want to say that I'm sorry. I know that doesn't change much, but for what it's worth…"

"You had no idea. In fact, how could any of us have known?" Olive answered for the group; it wasn't an acceptance of Melinda's apology, but it did acknowledge the situation they all found themselves in. "What are we going to do now?"

It was a question that all of them were asking themselves, but one that no one had any clue of how to answer. If they 'gave up', would it be in time to avoid the masses of the undead coming in their direction? Were they safer inside the building? Their choices weighed heavily on their collective minds, but none of them felt safe to answer the question that had been asked.

Accepting defeat, Melinda opened her jacket and removed the fake bomb. Laying it down on the table, she avoided the eyes of the group around her. "Don't worry, it's fake."

***

Lucas made his way toward the bank. He was on a collision course with the carnage, but he hoped that he could reach the bank before the zombies did. Once that happened, it would be hell on earth and there was no way that he would be able to get to her. That singular thought propelled him down the street on his motorcycle. He didn't care what laws he was breaking, he just wanted to get to her.

Thankfully traffic was light, most people opting to stay inside after the reports started to flood the news markets. There were a few crazies with their signs telling the world it was 'end of times', but Lucas didn't have time to warn them to get inside or out of town.

Sporadically he would see them if he looked down the cross streets before proceeding through an intersection. The attacks themselves were horrifying, but thankfully he didn't see much of what occurred before he moved on. The closer that he got, the more anxious he became. Lucas had no idea what he would do once he got to the bank and it was unlikely the police were going to let him walk up to the door and collect Melinda.

But still he had to try. That's what you do when you're in love.

***

The screams from the front of the bank told them it had reached them. Some in the group started to cry, while others rushed to the front doors to see it for themselves. Despite the images on the television, the situation was too incredible to be believed outright. There were those of them that needed to see it.

It was awful.

Men, women, and children in all states of dismemberment and shades of red littered the street in front of the bank. They were attacking the large assemblage of officers, biting them, eating their flesh. The police didn't even have the opportunity to fight back. Or the knowledge that fighting back was their only chance at survival.

The seven faces plastered against the glass of the doors watched it all in silence, noting the ferocious way the undead attacked and the voracious way the new converts rose from the asphalt. It was a cycle that none of them wanted to be a part of, and yet here they were witnessing it.

Melinda turned from her front row seat and moved to the wall, sliding bodily down it. She held her head in her hands and scratched her scalp. With the problem of the police gone, she still had to contend with the army who wanted to assimilate her into their ranks. And, unlock the door.

It was long minutes before any of them spoke.

"They're moving away." Raphael, the security guard, was the one to give the news.

Melinda stood up and turned to look outside. The ground was splattered with blood and ichor, and a few bodies remained, lying prone and still on the ground. The street was a mess; it looked like a war had been waged and won, the victors moving on to collect their bounty. It was all that she could do not to cry.

"What's that?" Olive asked as she pointed one of her long, manicured fingers toward the blue trailer emblazoned with the words command center. The slightest hint of movement could be seen on the door as it shook and bulged outward. "Is there someone still inside do you think? Maybe they can help us?" The expectant look on her face was hard to miss as she stared out the glass excitedly.

"Maybe we'll be saved!" Raphael hopped on the band wagon with her.

Melinda didn't have the heart to point out that any living person would have been able to open the door without a problem. Instead, she kept quiet and turned toward the conference room; there was nothing left to see outside.

She'd almost made it all the way to the back again before she heard the rumble. Thinking her mind was playing tricks on her, she continued into the back of the bank.

"Hey! There's a guy on a motorcycle coming. Maybe he can help us!" Once the words were out of Olive's mouth, Melinda spun back around and hurried toward the doors.

It couldn't be, could it? She thought to herself. Craning her neck, she tried to look down the street in the direction everyone else was looking. Her heart swelled when she saw him: Lucas! He had come to help her. In that moment, she knew that despite all of their problems, all of their fights, he truly loved her.

***

Lucas drove his bike up onto the sidewalk in order to skirt the barricades that had been erected around the entrance of the bank. He wasn't sure what he was going to find past all of the police cars, but it didn't look like there was anyone around.

Coming to a complete stop in the centre of the cordoned area, he got off his bike and engaged the kickstand. He could see the doors to the bank on his left and the people that were plastered up against it.

The ground around him was slippery with blood and tissue and Lucas watched his step as he looked for signs of any remaining zombies. From the looks of it, they had moved on, leaving ample food behind. Something must have drawn their attention away and he was thankful for it.

Walking up to the bank, he could see Melinda framed in the doorway, her mascara running down her face and the smile that warmed his heart. She was still alive. Realizing that she had not come running out of the bank at his arrival told him something was amiss. Not knowing what it was, he stopped a few feet from the door, a questioning look branded across his face.

"Are you coming?" He mouthed the simple question.

"We're locked in. The police are supposed to have a master key, but I don't even know where you would begin to look for it. I'm sure we can break the glass though." Melinda was ecstatic to see him and wanted to be out of the bank as soon as possible.

"Stand back!" Raphael said the words as he hefted the closest of the silver garbage cans in the air and brought it down against the pane of glass. The reverberation travelled up through his arms, causing him to drop the can on the floor with a clatter.

The glass didn't even have a scratch in it.

"Where should I look for the key?" Lucas had that way about him; instead of cursing bad luck, he put his mind to work finding an alternative.

"What was the manager wearing today Olive?" Melinda figured that if her body was one of the ones still in the street, perhaps the keys would be in her purse or on her person.

"She had on a navy pantsuit with a purple blouse. Why?" She asked the question just before a look of understanding crossed her face, "She also had blonde hair and was wearing flat shoes today. Her purse is big and black and has one of those scarf things tied around the handle."

"Thanks Olive," Melinda said as she smiled at her. "Did you get all that Lucas? Think maybe you can find her?"

"I'll give it a shot." With the words said, Lucas made his way around to each of the unmoving bodies that peppered the street. Sometimes he was fairly quick in his dismissal of one, others time he spent long moments making sure it wasn't her.

The group at the window watched his every move. They wanted to leave the bank and he really was their only option for rescue. Twice it looked like he may have hit pay dirt, only to find out that the purse in his hands belonged to someone else. As the time ticked on, each of them got more anxious. It felt like it was taking forever, but in truth only a few minutes had actually passed.

Suddenly, Melinda remembered the backdoor. Chances are it would be locked as well, but no one had actually tried it. "Olive, can you show me the backdoor?"

"Sure, it's this way," she said.

With a look back at Lucas in the street, Melinda followed Olive into the back of the bank. As they travelled down the hallway that led to the backdoor, Melinda couldn't help but feel a small amount of elation. The love of her life had come to find her. With that kind of luck, nothing could hurt them now.

Okay maybe the undead could hurt them, but that was a different kettle of fish altogether.

At the backdoor, Olive turned the knob and pushed. It didn't budge. Laughing, she reached up and turned the deadbolt, "this might help!"

Melinda laughed along with her, until the moment that Olive tried the door again and it still wouldn't bulge. Their laughter died in their throats as the screams started from the front of the bank. Thinking that Lucas had found the keys, Melinda and Olive rushed back to the double doors.

The sight that greeted Melinda was horrible!

Lucas was plastered up against the glass, a huge chunk missing from his shoulder. On the ground close to the command centre laid a new body. Why hadn't she warned him to be careful of the door?

"Lucas! No!" Melinda plastered herself up against the glass, fighting to get to him, to comfort him, to offer what little support that she could.

"I'm sorry" Those were the only words he said as the light in his eyes blinked off. His body slid down the glass, leaving a thick trail of red blood down its length.

Melinda began to cry and slid down the glass beside him. Heart-wrenching sobs racked her body as he laid still, the side of his face still visible against the pane of glass. She placed her face against his and let her heartache fill the room around her. Escape could wait; right now it was time to mourn.

Unsure of how long she sat across the window from him, Melinda was surprised to see his hand start to move. Looking up, she stared straight into the milky white eye of her former love, his lips and teeth gnashing at the glass, his hands knocking on the barrier as they tried to grab her.

VANIER'S BLUEPRINT:
A ZOMBIE TALE

June 30.

The day before Canada Day. I was in my tidy, sun-filled kitchen prepping my famous pasta salad for the familial festivities the following day. As I stirred the mixture of al dente macaroni, cubes of summer vegetables, herbs, and creamy salad dressing, my attention drifted to the news being broadcast on the television in the next room.

As my mind fought to comprehend what I was actually hearing, I continued to stir the salad in disbelief. It wasn't until I heard the screams of the eyewitness video that the large wooden spoon clattered against the rim of the glass bowl.

As I stumbled into the living room, my eyes found the television's screen. The sight that awaited me was horrendous – like something you'd see in a Hollywood blockbuster. The news station had the clip on a continuous loop, stuck in a horrifying replay mode. I saw the same four minutes and thirty-four seconds over and over and over again. It was like an accident scene you couldn't look away from...

The video was shaky at times and showed the slow but steady approach of a foreign freight vessel on a collision course with the waterfront of Lake Ontario close to the Redpath refinery. Within the first minute of the footage, the vessel appeared to make what looked like a soft nudge against the edge of the metal and concrete of Queen's Quay. The resulting gash that opened up the darkly coloured exterior of the vessel just above the waterline was proof that the collision had been anything but gentle.

The crash itself was a disaster in the making; the sinking of the vessel would have meant the closure of Queen's Quay for quite some time. We would have been lucky if that had been the only thing to happen.

As the vessel sat hooked upon the wharf, its dark surface emblazoned with what appeared to be characters from the Cyrillic alphabet, many rushed to see if they could assist anyone aboard before it sank. They were dwarfed against the sheer size of the vessel, but they went to help anyway – I'd like to say that it was the Canadian way, but in truth, when disaster strikes, heroes of all kinds come out of the woodwork.

Their valour was not rewarded in kind.

At approximately two and a half minutes into the shaky video, you could tell that something had gone awfully awry. The men and women who had run towards the ailing vessel were now running back toward the camera, their arms gesturing in what could only be understood as a warning. They sought refuge any place they could find it.

Hiding did them no good, as what poured forth from the rent in the belly of the beast was devastatingly unimaginable. Hundreds of bodies spilled from the ship like baby spiders hatching from their egg sacks. Each one of them in various stages of decomposition; each one of them looking for flesh to consume, a vector to spread their fatal cargo.

Shortly after, the panoramic view of the carnage was replaced by the hurried flashes of pavement rushing by as the videographer frantically fled the scene. A few short moments later, the loop restarted; images of the vessel floating listlessly on a collision course with the wharf filling the screen again.

I sat down, unable to comprehend what I was actually seeing. Was it a hoax? Someone's sick idea of a joke? The news affiliate didn't seem to think so and after checking all of the channels on my television, it was strikingly apparent that no one had anything other to report. In the back of my mind, I knew the video had been placed on a continuous loop so that the employees of the stations could flee. Of that I had no doubt.

I'm not sure how long I sat there staring at the loop as it replayed over and over again. I was dumbstruck. Sure, I'd seen all of the movies, played some of the video games, heck I'd even read a few apocalyptic books, but none of it had prepared me for seeing the stark cold reality of what was happening. Could I really believe what my eyes had just witnessed?

Getting up slowly, I made my way back into the kitchen. My refuge. The place where I worked out all of my issues while preparing my favourite dishes. With the spoon back in my hand, I stirred the pasta salad as my mind worked out the impossibility of what I had just seen.

The cathartic cyclical motion helped to slow my rapid pulse. I could feel the calmness wash over me and with it came a level of resolve. There was no way that I was going to go down without a fight. Not sure that I could trust the reports I had seen on television, I decided to drive out to my parent's house just outside of the city.

Rationalizing that I didn't want to show up and look like an idiot, I packed a small bag and my pasta salad before leaving the house. There was no way in hell I was going to look like an idiot in front of my brother by showing up at my parent's house in a panic over what was sure to be an elaborate hoax – I'd never hear the end of it.

Ever cautious, I took a quick look out each of my windows into the street below. Nothing looked amiss, so I figured it was safe to venture outside. Picking up my bag and the big white Corning Ware bowl, I strode purposefully to my front door.

With my hand on the doorknob ready to turn it, I stopped for a moment to take a deep breath. As much as I didn't want to admit it, the video had really rattled me. Gathering the resolve to breach the barrier that my door represented, I wrenched the knob to the left and whipped open my door.

Fuck!

Sucking my breath deep into my lungs and dropping the bowl of pasta salad, I screamed as loud as I could and directly into the face of my older brother, Gavin. Honestly, I think I scared him more than he scared me. Had the situation been different, I'm sure I would have laughed and held both the moment and the scream over his head for years.

To find Gavin at my door threw me into a bit of a panic. He would not have come over unless something serious was going on; he hated my building, especially since his latest ex lived down the hall from me.

"Thank God you're still here Vivienne!" He never called me Vivienne unless something was troubling him.

"I was just about to leave for Mom and Dad's... What's got you so riled?" I knew better than to tell him I'd already seen the footage. If it was a hoax, he'd do his best to make me believe it was true. At this point, I wasn't prepared to show my hand.

"Did you see the footage? The boat that ran ashore at Queen's Quay? Shit, that was fucked-up!"

"Yes, Gavin. I saw the footage, but you know things like that get faked all the time. Don't tell me you're scared of a few people in makeup?" As my false laughter faded away, I could tell that whatever Gavin had seen had scared the life out of him. The nervous knot I had successfully unravelled earlier was back and with it, a serious feeling of foreboding.

"Viv, we've got to get out the city while we still can. I'm dead serious..."

His plea was cut off by a shrill scream on the ground floor below us. Gavin used both of his hands to forcefully propel me backwards and further into my apartment, closing and locking the door behind us. Quickly traversing the length of my apartment, he drew back the curtains and peered outside, his face a mask of concern and fear.

His fear was contagious and I found myself wringing my hands in an effort to expel nervous energy.

"What do you see Gavin? Anything?"

Slowly turning from the window, his face changed from one of fear to one of laughter, his mirth barely contained behind his broad lips. "Geez, sis, you should have seen your face when that lady downstairs screamed! Best fifty bucks I ever spent!"

"You asshole! Are you telling me you paid someone to scare me? That's low, even for you!"

"Aww. C'mon Viv, you know you would have tried the same thing if you'd thought of it first." He came over and placed his muscular arms around me in a subtle apology. I couldn't really fault him as he was right – if I'd thought of it first, I would have done the same thing.

"I'm heading out to Mom and Dad's now, Gav. If you want a ride, you're welcome to it. Otherwise, I guess I'll see you tomorrow at the barbeque."

As I turned to collect my things, I remembered the pasta salad that now covered the floor of my entrance way. Heading into the kitchen for a dustpan, I hesitated for a moment when I heard another scream. Turning around, noticing that Gavin had returned to the window, I asked aloud, "You got two screams for fifty dollars? How long were you planning on keeping the rouse up?"

"I only asked her to scream once..." With his forehead plastered up against the window, I saw the moment his body tensed. Not going to fall for it, again, I continued into the kitchen and retrieved the dustpan and brush from its place beside my refrigerator. Turning back, I could still see him watching the world outside.

"I'm not falling for it again Gavin, so you can drop the act."

Kneeling to brush the ruined salad into the dustpan, I placed the bowl to the side as I keenly listened to any movement from my living room. There was no way I was going to let him get the drop on my again. Standing back up, I turned around to find Gavin still at the window. Thinking he was just hamming it up, I went over to stand beside him, my eyes focussing on the street below us.

Pandemonium. That's really the only word I could use to describe the scene below us.

People were running in every direction. Some were even attacking others. In some areas the pavement was soaked in blood while in others, it pooled around the bodies of those that had fallen. I hesitate even now to call them bodies as in only a few short moments, I knew they weren't actually dead. How else could one explain corpses with limbs torn off and great gaping holes in their midsections actually getting back up to rejoin the fray of violence?

The contents of the dustpan dropped to the floor in a great wet flop that sent pieces of slimy pasta in every direction. My left hand found Gavin's and we stood there, immobilized by the terror that had become the view from my window.

I'm not sure how long we stood there, staring out the window, but in a moment of sudden clarity, one thought struck me. Without a shadow of a doubt, I knew we had to get out of the city. In the confines of the narrow streets, we'd be trapped and that was the last thing I wanted to be.

Squeezing Gavin's hand, I pulled him away from the window and toward the door. With my keys in one hand, and the dustpan in the other, I raised onto my tiptoes to look through the peep hole. Nothing - yet.

Looking back at Gavin, I could see that he was still a little dazed. Hoping that he was coherent, I shook him and spoke aloud, "Gav, we need to get out of here. Out of the city. Are you ready to get to my car?"

His eyes stayed limpid for a moment and then, as if a switch flicked back on, he was alert again. Setting his shoulders in some sort of resolve, he nodded to me and I checked the peep hole one last time.

The coast was still clear, at least for the moment. Opening the door to a world gone crazy, I pulled my brother through it and quietly stalked down the hall toward the stairwell. Fortunately for us, the stairwell led directly down into the enclosed underground garage beneath my building. We should be able to safely get to my car as long as the structure hadn't been compromised.

Lady Luck was smiling down on us and we managed to get to my car without any incident. Not to say that specific events on our mad dash to get to the car hadn't sparked a few heart-pounding seconds; especially when my neighbour from down the hall decided to retreat back to his apartment at the exact moment Gavin reached to open the door leading to the garage.

A short scream later, we had passed him and were making our way down the row of cars to my Prius. Okay, that's maybe not the first car you'd want to be driving in a dangerous situation, but it did have its benefits. I knew that I could get to my parents without having to stop for gas – how many of you can say that you filled up the day before the Apocalypse?

Reaching the car seemed somewhat anticlimactic; we shared a nervous laugh before we decided what to do next. We agreed that a specific route was probably a bad idea; no telling what roads had been closed or what was clogged beyond movement. I lived closest to the Bathurst Street end of Little Italy, so it seemed best that we just head north for as long as we could.

Moment of truth – actually getting out of the garage and into the street. I was afraid, but I knew that in order to escape the city, I had no other choice but to leave the safety of the garage behind. Gavin looked over at me and gave me a look that screamed *what are you waiting for?* The silent slap in the face was all I needed.

I started the car, noting the near silent purr and threw it into gear. As I inched out of my parking space, I could see that there was no one else in the modestly sized enclosure. No other cars were moving or in the process of leaving. In fact, all the spots were occupied, letting me know that the building above me was full of my neighbours; all of them waiting out the storm. I couldn't help but say a silent prayer for them, knowing in my heart that they'd already signed their own death certificates by staying.

Fluidly, I pressed the automatic garage door opener on my visor and waited until it was up just enough to squeak my car through. The noise of the mechanics hadn't attracted any of the Zombies. (Yes by this point I had rationalized that we were dealing with the Undead) I figured it was because the entrance to the garage was on the side of the building opposite the view from my front window. Knowing it would buy my neighbours only a little more time, I hit the button to send the door down again.

Traversing the streets was like driving through your worst nightmare. As a fan of horror movies, I admittedly got a thrill from being scared. But this was so very different. This was real! The reality of the situation hit me full in the face the minute the first person ran across the road in front of my car, full of terror from what was chasing her. I don't think she saw me; her attention focused solely on trying to get away. She didn't escape her pursuer, by the way.

Many of them didn't. It was awful.

As I made my way toward Bathurst, travelling slower than the posted speed limit, I was struck by how quickly the situation had gotten out of hand. Only an hour before, I had been watching the footage in my living room. Now the streets of Toronto were beginning to look like a scene out of

Dawn of the Dead... People running in every different direction with the undead chasing after them, cars strewn about the road abandoned in favour of travelling on foot, and the bodies of those that simply did not make it - the ones that were lucky enough to never rise again.

The strident chime of my cellphone startled both Gavin and I. Forgetting that I had it tucked into my purse, it's ringing unnerved me. Thinking that I didn't want to pick it up only to be begged by a friend for salvation, I checked the display before connecting. My mother. Worse.

"Hi Mom. I really can't-"

"Vivienne, please tell me you're with Gavin? I can't get him on the phone."

"Yes, Mom, Gavin is with me. We're on our way out of the city so I really can't talk at the moment."

"Hand the phone to Gavin and concentrate on driving."

"Hi Mom." A pause followed as Gavin listened to our mother. "Yes Mom."

More silence.

"Okay, Mom. I've got it."

A longer pause.

"Yes Mom, I love you too. Tell Dad I love him." A small pause, "Okay, I got it. Sheesh Mom. I'm not stupid you know."

A smaller pause.

"Okay Mom, I'm hanging up. Bye!"

A small, short tone signalled that Gavin had disconnected from our mother. The funny thing about their conversation is that I know exactly what my mother was saying on the other end. Do this, don't do that. It was always the same thing; parents never truly believe their children can survive without their guidance. We'd gotten this far hadn't we?

"Mom says to head straight to the high school."

"What?" I honestly hadn't been expecting that.

"She said to go straight to the high school."

"Yes, Gavin, I heard what you said, I just don't understand why."

"She said something about a failsafe plan from the Forties. If she thinks that some old bomb shelter in the basement of the high school is going to save us from what's happening, I think she's finally gone completely crazy!"

"The Forties? She actually said the Forties? Geez, they are really losing it up ther-"

A hand smacked up against the window next to my face and I screamed, involuntarily jerking the car to the right and scraping up the side of a Civic parked on the street. Glancing right for a moment, I could see that I had pinned a body to the Civic, grinding flesh into the paint of both cars as I inched forward. I slowed for a moment, debating on what to do. Did the hand belong to someone that needed help? What about the person that I had pinned? I looked left only to be rewarded with a grimacing face, stuck in the act of mastication, covered in blood and macerated tissue. The sight made me cower away, pressing my foot a little harder on the accelerator; the body to my right forgotten in my haste to escape.

Leaving the scene behind as a reminder of what we didn't want to become, we slowly made our way out the city. It was a long drive up Bathurst, one that should not have taken us five and a half hours, but given the state of the roads and the top speed at which I could drive, we were lucky to get out at all. We left the living and the dead behind us, but managed to bring some of the undead north with us, at least part of the way. They followed us because we were moving and only dropped off when they found an attainable, slower moving source of food. I felt like the Pied Piper of Death; the soft hum of my Prius the tune that carried them along. Thinking I would continually look into my rear view mirror and see the trailing horde, I glanced up to find the roadway behind me curiously empty of mobile corpses. Had they decided that chasing us was no longer worthy of their effort? As much as I was glad to see them go, there was something altogether unnerving about being rid of them.

With the loss of our followers came the relative clearing of the roads. This far north, there were less cars, and even fewer people. Had they seen the devastation in the city and moved themselves farther out of reach?

Nearing the state of exhaustion, I turned right onto Bloomington and was thankful that my parents were less than an hour away. I wasn't sure how long it would take us to get into Uxbridge, but with the roads appearing to be less congested, I was confident it wouldn't be too arduous a drive from here.

As we drove along, my brother kept an eye out for anything that may have slowed us down. It was dark by then, and if you've never been driving through a rural community at night, you cannot truly appreciate the depth of the darkness. There were times that we travelled underneath street lights where other roads transected the one we were on, but the dampened glow of their fixtures only penetrated so far.

We moved more quickly along the road. It was odd at first, to see the roads relatively devoid of cars and people, but I quickly chalked it up to people having the foresight to leave and not get caught up in the pandemonium. I also knew that the five and a half million people living in the most densely populated regions of the GTA would keep the Zombies busy for as long as they were still moving. That presented yet another threat, since many would attempt to leave the city if they could, bringing the hordes with them into the outlying areas.

In the distance, I could see highway 404 as it stretched over Bloomington. I could see the illumination of the vehicles pointed north and the shadows of black that caused the headlights to flicker. Gridlock on the bridge under which I would have to pass. Was the flickering of the lights indicative of them?

The car slowed slightly in response to the subtle panic that was welling within my throat. Gavin grabbed my hand, a small reminder that we had a destination and that thankfully, I was not alone.

Setting my shoulders back into my seat, I accelerated with resolve. If the bridge was full of Zombies leaving the city, I certainly didn't want to be a sitting duck for them. Approaching the bridge, you could make out the faintly jerky movements of the undead. They had followed the exodus of cars northward. It was hard to tell if they were actually finding victims or only terrorizing those still locked in their cars. With traffic at a complete standstill and the bodies of the dead walking alongside the cars, I was sure that highway 404 would become a vehicular graveyard within a few days.

Once you ran out of gas on the highway, there was no way that you would be able to escape. Not with them waiting outside to consume you.

As we passed under the bridge, we could hear the desperate sound of horns. Didn't they realize honking wasn't going to help, that it would only draw the undead that were lingering around closer? Exiting on the other side, my brother and I both screamed as a heavy weight dropped onto the roof of my car, accompanied by a sickening crunch of bone. Not wanting to find out what it was, I accelerated quickly, hoping that the increase in speed would be enough to dislodge whatever had landed there.

As we neared the traffic light of the next crosscutting street, I knew that I would have to proceed with caution. There was no telling if any other cars would be careening up the road and I couldn't risk a crash, especially not this close to the highway that was funneling the Zombies north.

I slowed down, hesitating more than stopping. Gavin and I frantically looked both ways for anything resembling a speeding vehicle. Not seeing anything coming from either direction, I shot my car forward and across each of the four asphalt lanes.

The inertia from the quick acceleration dislodged the passenger from the top of my car. In my rear view mirror, I could make out someone standing in the intersection, the haze from the lights above proving to us that the individual was not dead yet. Stopping my car, thinking to help them in any way that we could, I started to reverse. It was at that exact moment that a large, yellow SUV plowed them down, likely mistaking them for one of the Zombies, or past the point of caring who they hurt in their haste.

The guilt overwhelmed me for just a moment. Someone had risked their life to ask for help and what had I done? Nothing.

"There was nothing you could do Viv... You had no way of knowing that what dropped onto the car was still alive. You can't beat yourself up over one death at this point, because if you did, you'd have to think of all the people we left behind in the city-"

"Okay that last part is not helping. Let's just get to Mom and Dad. We can figure out what to do after that, deal?"

"Deal."

The rest of the drive was uneventful. We saw few cars and those we did see were all heading north. I considered them the lucky ones, the ones that managed to get out. Of course we had no way of knowing if any of them had a plan other than to get out of the city or if they were travelling with anyone that had been infected. From what I had witnessed earlier, it didn't take long for the infection to spread once you were bitten, but then what did I know?

As we neared the outskirts of Uxbridge, we could see that most of the town was bereft of people. There were some random cars filling up at one of the three service stations we passed but other than that, it was a ghost town. Making our way deeper into town, we saw no one. Not even police cruisers patrolling the streets.

Turning onto Brock Street, Gavin glanced up at the façade of the town library. From the clock tower draped a fabric sign: Report to the High School Immediately.

"How are they going to fit all of the residents into the High School? There's got to be twenty or twenty-one thousand people..."

"What are you talking about Gavin?"

"The sign. It says 'Report to the High School'."

"Seriously? What are Mom and Dad getting us into?"

As we continued up the street, we could see the bright lights over the treetops. Coming over the last hill, the sight before us was impressive.

Barriers as high as twenty feet had been erected all around the high school with lights that shone into the sky as well as onto the ground. Armed guards stood along the top of the walls, each of them watching a different direction. I parked my car on the street and Gavin and I both got out, our jaws slightly agape at the sight before us.

One of the guards had noticed our approach and trained his rifle on us. The action didn't worry me; I knew that I was uninfected.

"Identify yourselves."

"I'm Vivienne Wilson and this is my brother Gavin. Is that you Steve? Steve Grant?"

"Vivienne Wilson? I haven't seen you since High School! How are you?"

"I've been better, to be perfectly honest... Is it possible for us to come in?"

"As long as you're willing to undergo a complete physical examination, the answer to that question is yes."

"Whatever it takes for you to let us inside, Steve."

With that, the door built into the side of the imposing structure opened and two men came out, both of them carrying rifles aimed directly at us. Leading us inside, we were stopped in an area that was completely sealed off from the rest of the interior.

Ordered to undress, we did exactly that. There were no privacy screens, but to be honest, I didn't even care. I was more concerned about getting into the compound and finding my parents.

"They're both clean. Unlock the inner door."

After hastily putting our clothes back on, we entered the compound which hummed with activity. Gavin and I stared in awe as we saw what had become of our high school. The façade itself had been reinforced with steel plates and the second story roof was newly equipped with mounted machine guns, solar panels and the hint of glass enclosures. It was quite the change from my days of classes, band practice, and student government. Noticing that Steve had come down from his post along the wall, we walked over to where he stood.

"So what do you think of the changes?"

"It's different, that's for sure. Why are there all of these changes, these additions? When did all of this work happen, Steve?"

"Well, after the Mayor received the letter in 1945, the plans began shortly after. Most of what you see was implemented from the plans today."

"Letter?"

"Yes, but we can get to all of that once I've shown you around. Let's get to it."

Steve led us in through the interior of the school and gave us the grand tour starting with main level. The front offices had been transformed into Command Central, complete with computers, television screens, telephones, short wave radios, and a radio telegraph machine for Morse code. Both Gavin and I stared in shock at the set up.

"Do either of you have any skill on a CB radio or know Morse code?"

We both shook our heads, unable to express ourselves in words. The cafeteria was next, then the Wood Shop where there were men and women hard at work creating all sorts of things. Each of the classrooms along the lower level had been transformed into different types of manufacturing areas. In one, there was a variety of different aged people putting together various types of bullets; in another, men and women stitched large bolts of cloth into what looked like clothing, blankets and other assorted items.

Climbing the stairs, I couldn't help but wonder how they had gotten everything together in such a short period of time. It was only earlier in the day that the ship had crashed up against Queen's Quay. "How did you get all of this together in such a short time span?"

"This has taken years, Vivienne. You'll understand better when you've read the letter."

The upstairs classrooms had been converted into bunk rooms while the science labs remained as classrooms. It was an awesome sight; my former high school had been transformed into a self-sustaining community. Everywhere we went, there were people: working, talking, being kids.

Next, Steve took us into the basement, showing us the biggest surprise of all. In the old part of the school, the part that had been built in 1923, the gymnasium had been located on the bottom level, and while we had been attending the school, the 76th Regiment of the Army Cadets had used the space for their meetings, drills, and storage. Only a select few knew what had been secretly taking place behind the large double doors set into the far wall.

Not only was it a stockpile of preserved goods, equipment, and every other supply you could possible think of, but there were also water filtration systems, generators, and batteries for storing solar power. The cavernous room stretched as far as the eye could see, with doors that lead off like the spokes of a wheel in each direction.

"What's behind all of the doors?"

Gavin asked the question as he looked around, his eyes as wide as saucers. Taking in the entire room was difficult; trying to wrap my head around the complexity of what we were being shown was harder. Steve's reply floored us even more.

"Everything. A completely self-sustaining environment designed to allow the citizens of Uxbridge Township the ability to live underground for a lengthy period of time should the need arise. The plans for the compound started in the forties, just after the war and have continued to expand and diversify since then. It was built piece by piece and updated as new technologies became available. There are a number of other compounds like this that we know about; other communities that took the letter to heart as well."

"What's this letter you keep referring to?"

"There will be time for that in a moment, I think there are some people who would like to say hello first."

With that, Gavin and I turned to see our parents, both of them aged beyond their years since we last saw them.

"Thank the Lord you both made it!"

My mother enveloped the two of us into a hug, while my dad hung back, never being the demonstrative type, even in a crisis. Breaking contact with my mother, I turned back to Steve.

"Okay, I want to know all about this letter. What did someone say that would have provoked such a response in Uxbridge of all places?"

"Oh, it's not just Uxbridge. There's a network of five hundred and forty two compounds similar to this built in towns and municipalities across Canada; each one of them self-sustaining and ready for any number of disasters."

"Five hundred and forty two? Seriously? That must have been some letter…"

"It was. Are you ready to understand why this place exists?"

"Absolutely!"

Steve led us out of the stockpile and up the stairs into what had been the main entrance to the school for sixty years. The walls of the entrance had always paid homage to the men and women who lost their lives during the Second World War. I had looked at the bronze plaques many times, reading the names and wondering who they might have been, silently acknowledging the sacrifices they made. It was an austere section of the school and one that most students treated with respect.

As I looked at the wall of bronzed plaques, I could see that an addition to the lineup had recently been made. Etched in striking relief were these words:

TOP SECRET

August 23, 1945

With the defeat of the Axis powers, the declassification of TOP SECRET documents out of the Soviet Union has created a situation unlike any we have ever encountered. Scientists, at the behest of their government, sought to create a biological weapon that would sway the tides in favour of the Allied Forces. With that creation, came a very serious threat to mankind. The biological weapon that was created has proven to have grave consequences; a very serious and fatal threat to the very world we have been trying to protect. All samples have been destroyed but the lasting effect on the populace remains to be seen. One small town in the north of the Soviet Union was wiped out, eradicated in an effort to stem the sweeping sickness that would have taken root. The Russians could not have known what they were going to achieve and as a result, many had to die for the knowledge they attained.

We were lucky this time, but no one knows if the threat has been truly vanquished. With this missive, I beseech you all to take heed and protect yourselves against what could be a coming threat. The best advice that I can offer at this time is to prepare yourselves against an enemy that is heartless, tireless and quite frankly, dead. If this weapon were to be unleashed upon the world again, I fear that humanity will quickly fall and be eradicated.

Take heed, and maybe, just maybe, we will persevere.

Sincerely,

Georges Vanier, Canadian Ambassador to France

MUST LOVE ZOMBIES

"Are you sure this is a good idea?" Arnold asked the question as he tightened the blue pinstripe tie around his neck.

"Arn, lose the tie! You kidding me? A tie? Tonight of all nights?" Louis shot him an exasperated look as he checked himself out in the bathroom's mirror.

"Sorry man, you're right. I don't know what I was thinking... Guess I'm just nervous. I've never done anything like this before." With one last look in the mirror over his dresser, Arnold turned to present himself to his best friend. "How do I look?"

"Like a lady killer!" Both men dissolved into nervous laughter and tried not to look at each other. Their anxiety crowded the room with an uneasy feeling akin to the first boy-girl party one would have attended while in middle school.

"Okay, time to get going Arnold. The ladies await!" Grabbing his winter jacket from the arm of the grubby Lazy-boy, Louis made his way to the front door of their apartment, checking his pockets one last time. Not finding what he was looking for, Louis walked back over to the computer and grabbed a piece of paper, folding it before putting it into the pocket of his jeans. Looking back at Arnold, who still stood in the doorway of his bedroom clutching his red parka to him like a stuffed toy, he asked, "ready?"

"Lou, I'm not sure if I can do this... I mean c'mon, how safe is it?"

"The website promised that all safety precautions including background checks have been taken. You've got nothing to worry about. People do this all the time. They advertise on the internet for fucksake – it can't be all that dangerous if it's on the internet."

Biting his lip, Arnold continued to stare at Louis, his eyes mirroring the weight of his options.

"Save that for the ladies, buddy. Now let's get moving!"

With a final doubtful stare, Arnold walked the short distance across the room and out the door. Unsure of what to expect, he decided to at least give it try. Maybe it wouldn't be all that bad. Things had certainly changed in the past fifteen years...

***

It all started with the routine flu shot. No one thought anything of it until people started to get sick. Really sick. So many people died in those first few weeks; innocent people that trusted the government.

In the end, it was the government that suffered. They were ill-equipped to deal with an unwanted side effect of the flu strain they had mutated. A mutation that reanimated the dead, causing them to walk among us again.

The problem wasn't so much that the dead had risen; they weren't the blood thirsty and brain hungry zombies that we had been raised to believe would plague us at some point.

Instead, they rose with a healthy dose of common sense and a lot of anger.

In fact, it gave rise to quite a few needs on their part and because the government had caused the problem, they had to pay for it. It would have been one thing if they had woken up hungry for the taste of human flesh. But when they could walk and talk better than some of the politicians in Washington, it was another story altogether.

Over the years, those that hadn't been killed in existentially-motivated attacks or who couldn't face life on earth for an eternity were able to petition the government for equal rights under the law. It wasn't an easy road, but many of the interest groups had helped to pave the way for them. Plus there was always the chance they could turn ravenous if they weren't given what they wanted. The government just decided it was best to placate them while figuring out a way to eradicate them.

That sparked a serious debate in itself: is there such a thing as duplicate genocide?

As the years passed, new cosmetic techniques were invented to keep the dead preserved and businesses catering to the existentially-challenged flourished. It was a great time to be an embalmer or mortician; business had never been better!

There were some out there who thought the entire affair was a travesty. The dead should be dead, not walking around or having a meatshake at the local diner. They lamented often and loudly over the fact that the dead should simply cease to exist except in memory and wanted them rounded up, put in concentration camps. It was a horrible time that split much of the nation.

But as time went on, seeing the dead on the street became somewhat normal.

***

"Do you know where you're going?" Arnold asked the question from the front of Louis' electric car. The silence of the engine unnerved him, but it was better than riding his bike. Certain neighborhoods had gotten a little more dangerous in the past year or so.

Some people said the attacks were perpetrated by the dead, while others maintained it was the living engaged in a smear campaign. Not wanting to learn firsthand which faction it really was, Arnold had stopped going out after dark. It was a small price to pay for safety.

"Yes. It's over on Vermouth, by the Multiplex. You know that club in the warehouse?" Louis spoke while concentrating on the road, his eyes never leaving the pavement rolling under his car.

"Isn't that a dump? I thought they condemned it a few years ago?" Arnold rubbed absentmindedly at his left eye, hating that he was only making the slight twitch worse.

"Nah, someone bought it and fixed it up. Now it's a club again." He turned to smile at Arnold, briefly flashing his perfect white teeth. "Hey, cheer up. Everything will be fine. Besides, you need to get laid man! How long's it been anyway?"

Feeling his face flush at the mention such a private topic, Arnold stared out his window a moment before answering, "three years. Before Jenny left at least."

"Seriously? Man, you do need to get laid!" Louis laughed as he made the comment, thinking to himself he'd be lucky enough to see some action himself. Times were tough these days. With the advent of new preservation techniques, many of the dead were looking better than the living and that certainly didn't help the numbers when it came to dating. Turning the car into the parking lot, Louis selected a space and then turned off the engine. Sliding the keys out of the ignition, he checked his hair one last time in the rearview mirror. "Ready?"

Getting out of the car was one of the last things Arnold wanted to do, but he'd promised Louis so he did it anyway. Besides, he did need to get laid and perhaps this was his best option.

Walking up to the club, a garish banner told of the event to take place inside – Living/Dead Speed Dating. If Arnold could have crawled inside himself to die, he would have. Around the entrance of the club a few people lingered, holding signs protesting the event. Louis hadn't said anything about this kind of attention...

"Maybe we shouldn't do this? Look at the people! What if there's a riot or something?" Clasping his parka to his chest, Arnold chewed on his bottom lip nervously.

"Watch it Arn, you'll chew that thing off if you're not careful! Look, let's just go inside and see what it's all about. If you're still nervous, we don't have to stay. Deal?"

"Okay Louis, you've got a deal."

As they made their way to the front door, amid the sounds of discourse and strife from the protestors, a large man asked for their names. Louis gave them quickly, hoping to get Arnold inside before he lost his cool and his nerve. Their names checked out and they were soon whisked into the interior of the club. Thankful they had brought the jackets as suggested, they put them on and walked deeper into the event.

A few men lingered around the room, talking to each other and sipping on overpriced drinks. The center of the room was set up with fifteen tables, each of them overlaid with a red tablecloth and set with two chairs. Candle flickered on the tables, giving the dim room a romantic feel. The only thing out of the ordinary was the temperature. It felt like a freezer.

"Louis, where are all the women?" Arnold asked as he blew on his hands to warm them up.

"The site said that they don't let the ladies mix with the men before the event starts. The organizers want all of the impressions to be true first impressions or something like that. They'll be here shortly though, so don't worry." Louis' confidence was starting to show through his own slight anxiety. Neither of them had ever done anything like this before.

Before either of them could speak again, a tall man wearing a long pewter colored pea coat came to stand in front of the bar. He clapped his hands once and waited for the ambient noise in the room to quiet before speaking.

"Welcome to Living/Dead Speed Dating. My name is Hank Azreal and I will be your host. The rules are simple: you will have five minutes to talk to each of the ladies present. In that time, it is your responsibility to make yourselves sound interesting. At the end of the night, each of you will score the ladies out of ten and then mark down whether or not you would like to see them again. The ladies will do the same thing. If there are any mutual matches, you will receive the number or numbers of the ladies that would also like to meet you. What you do after that is entirely up to you. Are there any questions?" Azreal clasped his hands together as he looked about the room, seeking out any questions that may need to be answered. "If there's nothing else, let's begin!"

With a quick clap of his hands, a set of double doors at the back of the club opened and fifteen women entered the room, each of them walking to what Arnold assumed were assigned tables. The women wore party dresses in a wide range of colors and from afar you'd never really be able to tell they were dead. Once all the ladies were seated, Azreal called upon the men to each take a seat.

Arnold was one of the last men to find an empty spot in front of one of the women. It was all he could do not to stare at her. With a clap of the hands, the timer began and Arnold was left to his own devices.

"Hello," she smiled. "My name is Bethany. Nice to meet you." The woman seated across from him was diminutive, almost childlike in stature. She sat there wearing a stunning royal blue satin dress that showed off her shoulders and complimented the milky hue of her eyes. Her copper colored hair was swept up in a loose bun and tendrils of curls spiraled down to splay across the pale, dark veined flesh of her décolletage.

"I'm Arnold. Pleased to meet you ma'am." In his nervousness, Arnold was the consummate gentleman.

"So Arnold, what brings you here today?" Bethany asked the question in an innocent way, so gentle in her request that Arnold couldn't help but answer honestly.

"I'm not entirely sure. My friend thinks I need a woman in my life, and to be honest, I do miss that. But I'm not looking to rush into anything really. My last girlfriend left me for another man, a dead one."

"I'm sorry to hear that Arnold. Before the mutation, my boyfriend cheated on me with another woman. I didn't much care at the time to be honest though; he was as boring as they come!" Bethany smiled again, displaying small white teeth.

Arnold smiled back and his unease with the situation melted away. "What brings you to this event Bethany? Surely, you don't need any help finding men."

Bethany giggled for a moment, "you'd be surprised. Many of the men out there either don't like the dead, or the dead ones are no longer capable of certain sexual acts. It does break you know, eventually anyways." Realizing that she had spoken about such an intimate topic, her right hand flew to her face, an act that would have hidden her blush had her blood still be flowing. "I'm sorry; I should never have said that!"

Reaching out his hand, he laid it on top of her left hand, noting the cool chill that emanated from it. "It's okay, don't stress about it."

For the rest of the allotted time, Bethany and Arnold engaged in a flirtatious game of small talk, each of them staring intently at the other. It wasn't until the man whose turn it was to sit and talk to Bethany for the next five minutes touched him on the arm that they even realized their time was up. Moving to his right, Arnold sat down at a table across from a buxom blonde in a tight black dress. He made small talk, but didn't have the connection with her that he'd experienced with Bethany. There was just something about her that made his pulse race.

The rest of the dates went similarly. No one caught his attention the way that Bethany had and he really hoped that she felt the same way. Despite his apprehension at coming to the event, he was glad he'd made the effort as a small ball of excitement built in his stomach.

Waiting at the end of the event was torturous. The ladies had all been escorted back to the second room to make their evaluations while the men made theirs. There was only one woman that Arnold wanted to meet again and the wait was killing him.

Louis on the other hand was raving about his numerous love connections. From the way that he was talking, one would have assumed his intent was to collect a harem for his personal usage. His chatter was non-stop and as he dissected each of the women in a salacious way, Arnold barely listened. Until he heard Bethany's name.

"Dibs on Bethany man."

It was a simple statement, but one that spoke to Arnold's desire for her.

"Sure Arn, no problem." Louis took one look at Arnold's face and decided it was better to just let it be than to question him further. Besides, he knew that Bethany wasn't the cream of the crop anyway. He was okay with Arnold calling dibs, especially since there were lots of other ladies to go around.

Arnold waited the tense thirty minutes while Azreal tabulated the potential matches, chewing on his bottom lip and fantasizing about Bethany. All he wanted to do was learn more about her, and maybe perhaps if she let him, kiss her. He wondered what it would be like to kiss her. Would her lips feel funny? Would they be cold? Before he knew it, Arnold had worked himself up into a frenzy of arousal.

Thankfully, before Arnold could completely disgrace himself in front of the other guys, Azreal came back to where they had gathered with the results of the night. Giving each of the men a sheet of paper, he reminded them the ball now lay in their courts. They could choose to call any of the women on their lists, but he warned them all to be respectful and careful. "Safe sex gentlemen, safe sex!"

Arnold was nervous to see if there was a number on his sheet. He'd only expressed an interest in one woman, so if her name and number weren't there, no one's would be.

Slowly he turned over the sheet, afraid to find it blank Arnold closed his eyes, prolonging the tension of anticipation. Carefully, he peaked through one of his lids and was rewarded with a name and a number.

Bethany wanted to see him again too! Arnold was elated. He felt like he could have danced out of the club and not given a shit about who saw him. With a smile from ear to ear, he turned to Louis.

"Any takers?" he asked.

"Yeah, I've got a few numbers to call. I might just play it safe and call them all," with a wink, Louis nudged Arnold in the arm. "What about you? Get any bites?"

"I got one, and one is all I need." Arnold stared dreamily into Louis' face, caught up in the moment of discovery.

"Good for you man, good for you."

***

Three days later Arnold was set to meet Bethany for dinner. Not having wasted any time once he got home, Arnold called her and asked her out on a proper date. He wasn't sure how the dinner date was going to work, but he'd been assured by the maître d' of the restaurant that they could cater to the needs of the living and the dead. Nervous, he paced the lobby of her building before he rang the buzzer for her apartment.

Thoughts ran through his head. Over and over. He wasn't afraid of being with a dead woman, but he was afraid of the prejudices that still plagued inter-existence couples. As much as he tried not to build things up in his mind, he was afraid of some of the consequences he may have to face. While being dead wasn't as discriminatory as it used to be, there were still many that didn't understand.

Setting his resolve, Arnold rang the bell. Bethany answered within a heartbeat, asking him if he wanted to come up for a drink before leaving. Accepting her offer, he waited for the elevator, drawing his suit jacket closer around his body in the chill of the corridor.

Reaching Bethany's apartment, he knocked quietly on her door. When she answered, she was wearing a gorgeous floor length gown in red silk. Her hair was left down to float about her shoulders in copper waves and to Arnold she had an ethereal glow. In that moment he realized just how much he wanted to be with her.

"Hello Arnold, how are you tonight?" The breathless way that she whispered his name was arousing.

"I'm very well, thank you. How are you Bethany?" He wanted to take her into his arms immediately, but stopped himself with sheer willpower. Even her scent was intoxicating, a subtle combination of disinfectant and formaldehyde with robust floral accents. He felt his body stirring but willing it silently to behave itself.

"Glass of wine?" She offered the alcohol as she moved into her apartment. It wasn't overly large, but it was well appointed. A small table sat against a wall, with two chairs on either side of it, a plush sofa took up another wall and it was framed with bookshelves that reached the ceiling, full to the brim with interesting spines. A flat screen TV sat opposite the sofa and next to it was a door that lay partially open. Through the door, Arnold could see a king-sized bed and on it a lacy black nightgown. He swallowed quickly in reaction to the nightgown.

"Umm... yes please. Red if you have it." Arnold smiled and turned to take in the view from the large glass doors that separated her balcony from the living room.

Feeling her come to stand next to him, he turned his head and accepted the proffered glass of wine. Sipping it, he was taken aback by the quality. "Do you always serve such fabulous wine?"

"Always. Before the mutation I was a connoisseur, but now the stuff just tastes like garbage to me. I find that good wine helps to dispel nerves." Once she was done speaking, Bethany giggled and covered her mouth in such a way that it made Arnold gush even more. He was smitten and fairly certain that she knew it. Taking the now empty glass from him, she asked "ready to go?"

"Absolutely."

Dinner was an interesting but enjoyable affair for Arnold. He had no idea what the dead ate, but when he saw that Bethany had ordered *steak tartare*, he realized that her tastes were truly quite refined.

As they talked and laughed, all under the guise of getting to know one another, Arnold couldn't stop the feeling of contentment that coursed through his body. He was blind to the stares of other diners and missed many of the rude comments that were directed at their table.

Once dinner was over, as they were walking to his car, Bethany asked Arnold if he wanted to come up to her apartment when he dropped her off. Excitement coursed through his body as he accepted the offer, contemplating what it would be like to kiss her for the first time.

Arnold didn't have to wait very long, for as he was opening the passenger side door for Bethany, she raised herself on to her tiptoes and placed her lips on his.

The moment was electric. Her lips turned warm as his played across them, but the contact was over too soon. Bringing her hand up to touch her full bottom lip, Bethany smiled before getting into the car.

Back at her building, desire sparked between the pair as they rode the seventeen floors up to Bethany's apartment. In the confines of the cool small space of the elevator, their bodies barely touched along the length of their arms, but even the minute contact lit his nerves on fire. He wondered if she felt the same sort of reactions as him and almost asked her. His fear of ruining the moment held his words back; the last thing he wanted to do was offend her and he really had no idea what was politically correct where the dead were concerned.

Taking her keys out of her purse, Bethany was the first to leave the elevator, her body drawing Arnold out as well. He was like a lost puppy following the first nice person home. Walking down the hallway to her door was excruciating painful for him already, his desire evident to anyone that could have looked. Sliding the key into the lock, Arnold could hear all of the tumblers moving in slow motion and the agony of the wait was starting to wear on him. Never before had he wanted someone as much as he wanted Bethany.

Finally, the door swung open and she invited Arnold inside the climate controlled space that he barely noticed in his aroused state. All he could think about was the moment when he would finally be able to touch her. Closing the door behind him, and locking it for privacy, Arnold followed her deeper into the apartment. Once inside he stopped, suddenly unsure of what to do with himself.

Sensing his unease, she smiled and held out her hand. Arnold took it in his, loving the feel of her cool powdered palm against his. Bethany turned and led him into the bedroom, the gentle sway of her hips all that Arnold could concentrate on for the moment.

Once through the threshold, she turned to him and brought her body close to his. Her face was just inches from his and for the first time he truly began to notice the differences between them; the most startling of which was the absence of her breath on his neck as she stared up at him.

Dismissing the thought, he trailed his fingers up her arms all the way to her face. Cupping it between his hands, he brought his mouth down to hers.

The moment their lips touched nothing else seemed to matter. If Arnold was a betting man, he would have put all he owned on the fact that he had fallen in love with her. Not able to judge her feelings just yet, Arnold at least was able to realize that she was kissing him back, her urgency feeding his own. Drawing back from the kiss for a moment, Bethany fought to keep herself composed.

"I just need a minute in the washroom to take care of a few things. I'll be back in a minute or two." After making her request, she disappeared from the room, taking the nightgown with her and leaving Arnold to figure out what to do.

Unsure of himself, he sat down on the edge of the bed, noting that it was soft and somewhat cool through the fabric of his pants. He could hear Bethany in the washroom; water running, the spray of something like perfume, normal sounds one would expect to hear. When the water turned off, Arnold heard the click of the light switch and the door opening.

Bethany came back into the bedroom dressed in the leave-nothing-to-the-imagination nightgown. It was long and black, made from a sheer lace that covered everything but not by much. She was a vision and Arnold was having trouble controlling himself. Standing up, he took her gently into his arms, loving the feel of her body against him, kissing her with reckless abandon.

Taking charge in the moment, Bethany broke the kiss and placing one hand on his chest, she motioned for him to wait. Slowly, she slid his jacket over his shoulders, allowing it to drop to the carpet below. Next she took her time with each of the buttons on his shirt, pulling it from the waistband of his pants before sliding it off to let it rest with his jacket. Her hands moved to the fly of his pants, undoing the button and drawing down the zipper, her fingers grazing his erection through the soft fabric of his underwear. In that moment, Arnold almost came undone with pleasure. Pushing him back onto the bed for a moment, she dropped to her knees to untie his laces and remove his shoes and socks. With that task completed, she stood back up and hooked her fingers into his waistband, drawing his pants and underwear down over his knees and feet. Lying back in all his naked glory, Arnold wasn't sure what she might do next, but by this point, he was truly past caring.

Dropping back to her knees in front of him, Bethany took his swollen erection in her hand and started to stroke it as her eyes stared up into his. Arnold was mesmerized. Her eyes were so big, so innocent and yet they held a mischievous quality that held him entranced. In the next moment, she had covered the tip with her mouth and Arnold very nearly came from the pleasure and pressure of her cool mouth. As she began to moan and suck in earnest, he laid back and enjoyed the feel of her mouth around him. Within a few minutes he was close to coming, her mouth never breaking contact and Arnold came to the realization that she didn't need to breathe. It was that thought along with the exquisite pressure of her lips and tongue that drove him over the edge. Exploding into her mouth, his body bucked him deeper into her throat.

With a gentle smile on her face, one that reached all the way to her eyes, she released the suction of her mouth and licked all the way up the length of his shaft. Standing up, she took the straps of her nightgown and pushing them over her pale shoulders, letting the lace trail slowly down the curves of her body. Fully exposed to him at last, Arnold could see the taut nipples of her large, firm breasts and the triangle of hair that sat between her hips.

Moving himself back on the bed, Arnold crooked his finger at her in an invitation for her to join him. Bethany got onto the edge of the bed and crawled catlike up to where he now lay, noting the swelling occurring between his legs again. Crawling up the length of his body, she straddled him, her breasts playing against his chest and her hair framing the sides of his face. Leaning down, she kissed him. It was primal and so god damned sexy; Arnold arched his body against hers in response, letting her feel his rock hard erection against her. Bethany moaned in response and breaking the kiss for a moment, she reached into her bedside table, removing a bottle of lubricant. Leaning back, she squirted a dollop onto the head of his penis and used her hand to spread it down the shaft. Using her same hand, she reached between her legs and smoothed some of the lubricant over her lips as well. Arnold watched in amazement – never before had he seen a woman touch herself and the glimpse of Bethany with her hand between her legs turned him on even more. Laying the bottle back on the nightstand, she pushed her body down on his, letting the tip of him enter her coolness.

At first, Arnold found the contact a little unnerving. She was so cold against the heat of him, but once she started to move her hips, fully taking him inside her, he forgot all of his concerns. As she moved her hips back and forth against his, he bucked up against her; the two of them moving in unison.

As the pleasure built for Arnold, he began to feel a strange tingling sensation over the length of his penis. It was like each of his nerves was firing at an exponential rate. The pleasure was intense and a little numbing. Looking up at Bethany, he could see her face contorting in pleasure, her body moving faster to make greater contact with him. Each time he felt a shock on his penis, he would feel the walls of her vagina quiver and Bethany would moan in ecstatic response. Not sure what was going on, but loving the new sensations over the length of his shaft he continued to push himself up into her.

Like lightening he came again, but the pleasure on his already sensitive skin drove him to continue thrusting. Arnold was almost on autopilot. He knew he was reaching for another orgasm, his third of the night, and while he felt selfish, he knew there was nothing he could do to stop himself.

The walls of Bethany's vagina were quivering like mad, her screams and moans of pleasure egging him onward and upward. With one final hard squeeze of her vaginal muscles, Bethany jerked and spasmed, screaming his name in the moment of her orgasm. Holding her hips against his, Arnold still bucked wildly, the pleasure between them almost too much. Mere moments after Bethany came, Arnold did as well, his breath coming in ragged gasps, the length of his penis still a quivering mass of pleasure tinged flesh.

Sliding his hand up her body to cup one of her firm breasts, he smiled into her face, a question in his eyes.

"First time with a dead girl?" Bethany asked the question as her body came down from the high of orgasm. Still straddling his deflating erection, she reveled in the feelings of sexual ecstasy.

"Yeah, it was. But it was amazing!" He pulled her down and reached his head up for a kiss, letting his mouth linger long on hers.

Giggling, she bit his lower lip and she suckled it. "I wish I could take all the credit babe, but it's my Must Love Zombies."

"Must Love Zombies?" Arnold's face was a conundrum of pleasure and confusion.

"Yeah. Must Love Zombies. It's the only lubricant guaranteed to awaken the dead nerves of today's Zombie. At least that's what the commercial says…" Her voice trailed off as Arnold moved his hand between their bodies, his fingers snaking into her moistness.

"Is it edible?" he asked with a twinkle in his eye.

With her voice catching in her throat, she answered, "yes!"

Gently moving their bodies so that Bethany now lay beneath him, Arnold began to kiss a line down her chest and stomach, his hand reaching for the bottle on the bedside table.

FLASH FICTION DUO

FIGHT

It comes at me with a ferocious roar; its lips drawn to reveal sharp broken teeth. Stepping back, I'm met with hard resistance. Trapped! Unrelentingly it advances, jaws gnashing at the promise of a fresh meal. I raise my arms, weapon cocked and aim. My muzzle explodes and the body falls to the floor: bullseye.

HUNGER

Hunger; deep, painful hunger drives it forward. Milky eyes catch the hint of movement, drawing its attention to the meal standing, stunned, silent. It lurches forward, its intent to pursue ruthlessly. Luck, it seems is on its side; its prey cannot move. Trapped! Its hunger swells at the promise, but is met with swift denial.

EXIT

"It should just be around this rack Gavin. Hurry!" Catherine spoke in hushed tones, trying to propel her boyfriend into reacting faster.

The pair had entered the warehouse to look for supplies and had hit the jackpot! In both food and water.

They'd only been inside for a few moments, stuffing the absolute necessities into their canvas packs before they started to hear the thumping.

Gavin, being the more curious of the two, decided to check it out. He only got partway down the aisle before the crash reverberated through the warehouse.

Not knowing what was actually going on, Catherine grabbed their bags and hauled ass to where Gavin stood listening. Looking up she spotted the signs that pointed to the exit and started to navigate her way out, dragging Gavin behind her.

Pushing on the handle of the hollow metal door, she came up short, confusion written plainly on her face. Gavin thrust her awkwardly aside, putting his weight behind his attempt, panic setting in as the door remained completely closed. It wouldn't budge.

As they turned to look for a different exit, they saw the hordes slowly closing in…

BITE

"Fuck that hurts!" Mary gritted her teeth against the pain of the needle and turned to look at the partially finished butterfly on her wrist.

"Look sweetie, I warned you before I started that beauty is pain. Stop moving!" The gruff artist roughly grabbed her hand to move her wrist back into position.

A few more pricks of the needle was all she thought she'd be able to endure. Then, the pain stopped, along with the sound of the machine's motor.

"What the fuck?"

Mary opened her eyes and turned to face her tattoo artist, noting the puzzled look and the silence that now pervaded the room. Throughout the shop, she heard nothing; no other motors buzzing.

One by one, the clients and their artists gathered in the common area of the shop, each of them a little more confused than the next. The owner of the shop, a big burly guy with more ink than virgin skin, came into the room, telling everyone the fuse box was fine, that the power must be out.

Each of them looked out the big windows at the front of the shop, surprised by the pandemonium they could see.

Curiosity took over, winning against their better common sense, and the group moved to the front door. En mass they exited, wanting to see what was going on.

"Oww! That fucking idiot just bit me!"

FLICKER

With their perimeter set up, Sally and Joe settled into their sleeping bags around the fire. It was dangerous to have a fire out in the open, but it had been days since they'd seen one of them. They assumed they were safe, but there's never any security after the end.

In an effort to obscure what they had done, Sally and Joe had built a ring around the pit, placing the stones so they better concealed the flames. It made them feel safer and soon both of them had dozed off for the first time in months.

That was their second mistake.

As the pair slept, the flicker from the fire caught the attention of a walker in the woods. A lucky step over the can-laced rope and it was inside the perimeter, closing in on the sleeping lumps.

As the fire drew it forward, Sally and Joe continued to sleep, the sounds of contented breathing broken by the hideous keening.

Panicked screams followed as Sally valiantly tried to fight the creature off Joe, but it didn't do any good. The pair hadn't seen one walker in a few days but that night, three walked away from the fire...

HORSE

It neighed softly, fear flickering in its eyes. The poor animal was scared and with just cause.

A horde ringed its paddock, each of them straining against the wire fence, trying to get in.

It circled the inner sanctum, nervous energy twitching its muscles as it pranced. The undead surrounding it keened desperately for the meal only a few feet away.

The fence bowed slightly before snapping back, propelling part of the gathered group backward. With the wall of bodies behind them, they snapped forward again, the tension on the fence finally causing it to buckle inward. Like molasses, they flooded into the pasture, each of them slowed by the sheer number clamouring to get in.

As the undead sought out the entrance to their prey, the animal saw its chance.

With hands scrabbling to catch hold, it bolted in the opposite direction, barely clearing the fence as it jumped. Hands continued to grab at the fuzz-covered muscle as it mowed down any who stood in its way.

Clearing a copse of trees, it was brought up short. The numbers in front greatly outweighed those behind. Flight took over again and it bolted through the middle, only to be stopped by the sheer number of bodies packed tightly together.

Within moments it fell, its attempt at escape over.

BELOW

Above them they hear the shuffling, the halting steps over the rough boards. There is nothing they could do but wait them out.

A small, soft whimper escapes the lips of the smallest child. A hand roughly flattens itself across the offending mouth, startling her even more. A louder cry is somewhat muffled by the fingers but it's too late.

They've heard and are trying to locate the source of the noise.

Panic spreads quickly through the bodies cramped into the space, a palpable feeling that sets more nerves on edge and creates additional nervous energy.

The energy translates into more panic, and more panic into noise. They clamour from above is deafening as the dead scramble to get at the living.

There is nowhere to go but up. Their earthen cellar nothing but a tomb they now want to escape.

And then it is quiet. No sound, no scraping. Just the absence of noise.

It is the calm before the storm. The moment before the fall.

With a resounding crack, the wooden planks overhead crumble downward, pinning some, killing others. Pandemonium ensues as the living try to fight, but they have been relegated to the bottom of the food chain now.

AGONY

The pain is intense, searing as it travels through the network of my body. Each new invasion feels worse than the last but there's nothing my cells can do to fight them off. I'm succumbing to the army and my defences never had a chance.

I want to fight, but I know it'll do no good. Waging a war on the cellular level is do or die. And I'm about to die. But it's not going to be much of a death.

There was a time I never wanted to die. A time where I wished I could live forever. I would give anything at this point to simply die. That is not going to be my fate. I will come back but will act as a vessel for transmission. The army has only one goal – to conquer.

My new eyes open and I see the world from behind a milky haze. Now I search…

BLOAT

"What the fuck is that smell?"

"Shhh! It's got to be one of them! Don't tell it we're here for fucksake!"

Mark wasn't sure what to say at Amanda's outburst. But then he'd never actually been outside since it all went down. Sure he'd seen things from his window, but never anything up close. Hell he was surprised he'd even gotten this far…

As an agoraphobic, he hadn't set foot outside his home since he was twenty-one and at thirty-seven, when the zombies attacked, he was perfectly fine staying inside. Until his supplies ran out.

At least he'd had Amanda to count on. She was his only life line, even before the uprising. One night, after seeing the reports on the news, he'd heard her knocking frantically at his door. She'd come to try and convince him to leave his condo, but it had taken her four months.

With the undead moving out of the cities, she'd finally convinced him it was the safest time for them to move.

Not that it was an easy feat for him at all. They started slowly, having decided on a number of milestones to overcome each day. Some days Mark failed, not being able to get much past the front door but it all changed the day Amanda told him she was leaving.

And she did leave. The very next day. But it was good for Mark because it forced him to make a decision: to leave and try not to look back.

So on his first day outside, after stepping into what appeared to be an abandoned building, he found his olfactory senses assaulted with the concentrated smell of them. There had been whiffs as the travelled down the streets but nothing as bad as this.

Rounding a corner, trying to source the smell, they came upon a hulking mass of what used to be a man, his body so bloated it appeared to be twice the size.

Exhaling sharply at the smell, Mark exclaimed "I think I'm going to be sick!"

At the sound of a voice, the body rolled and the distended stomach burst, releasing a smell that burned their eyes and activated their gag reflexes. It started to crawl toward them, dragging its bulk with it.

Amanda turned to flee, but Mark's feet were rooted to the spot. He longed for his safe apartment and silently cursed Amanda for making him leave it.

ELBOW

It made contact with Jesse's nose as Frank spun around. They shouldn't be fighting, especially not out in the open, but that young prick had something coming to him.

"What the fuck you do that for?" Jesse whined as the blood poured from his nose. He stood in front of Frank, his hands held up in front of his face in the classic pugilist stance.

"You know why you stupid little shit."

"Are you seriously mad about that? It's not my fault she went out and didn't come back. I didn't put her on the recon team Frank."

Marta, Frank's wife, had been part of the recon team who'd been attacked yesterday by another group of survivors. Without gear and a lot of ground to cover before dark, they hadn't stood much of a chance in the confines of the city. Open territory would have been one thing, but with hardly any exits and too many places for the undead to hide, the city was a deathtrap.

Today, Frank had taken a small group into LA to look for his wife and the rest of the team. The look on his face said it all by the time they'd gotten back with Harry, the lone survivor.

"She wasn't supposed to be out there. It wasn't her team – it was yours. You didn't go so she ended up having to run back to back missions. If that's not your fault, I don't know what is." Frank reinforced his anger and blame with another well-aimed crack of his elbow, splitting the skin below Jesse's left eye.

"You can keep hitting me man, but that's not going to bring her back."

"I know, but it sure as hell will make me feel better!"

LOVE BITES:

A VALENTINE'S DAY MISADVENTURE

Sitting propped up against the bar, Kyle turned the viscous red liquid around and around the highball glass, his head supported by his other hand. Playing the part of maudlin vampire was something he did very well.

Tonight was no different than any other night. He'd made plans to meet Arielle for drinks and then maybe dinner if the mood came over them, but here he was sitting in the bar, still waiting for her after two hours.

Draining the crimson from his glass, he called out to Norm, "can I have another?"

Norm, the stodgy barkeep that kept this place alive despite all of his undead customers came to stand in front of him. "Don't you think you've had enough?"

"No," was all that Kyle could answer as his body slumped in utter dejection.

"You can't keep drinking yourself into oblivion each time one of them fails to show. You're drinking me out of all of my infused stock." Norm paused for a moment to fill the glass, "do you know how hard it is to convince drunks to donate these days? So many of them are belligerent and tend to revoke permission when they sober up…"

Norm's voice trailed off as he realized that Kyle was caught up in his own world. Knowing there was no use talking to him in this mood, he moved on to serve his other, more upbeat patrons.

Kyle continued to slump even lower on the stool, the rejection of the night deflating his normally overlarge ego. Noting the woman seated to his left two stools over, he turned a glassy stare in her direction.

From what he could see, she was a fairly ordinary woman. Perhaps a little plain in the face, she had a strong pulse in her neck that instantly attracted him. Perking up at the thought of salvaging his night, Kyle momentarily forgot about his woes and attempted to look dashing in his black velvet suit jacket, dark jeans, and slightly less than crisp white shirt. Mussing his shoulder length chestnut hair, he took a quick glance in the mirror behind the bar to gauge the damage. Satisfied, he turned toward her and smiled.

She didn't notice.

Continuing to smile, Kyle cleared his throat surreptitiously.

That didn't work either.

Wobbly standing on his long legs, Kyle moved to the stool next to her. Seating himself with his back to the bar, he leaned far enough back to be in her field of vision. Plastering a debonair smile across his lips, he waited.

For a long time.

"Can I help you with something?" The words, once they were spoken came out in clipped tones.

Continuing to smile despite his frustration at her attitude, Kyle introduced himself. "Hi, I'm Kyle. Would you like to chat? Perhaps let me buy you a drink?"

"I've got a drink, thank you." More of the same clipped tones.

"How about a chat then?" Persistent; you'd have to give him that one.

"I don't mean to be rude, but I would just like to be left alone. Thank you." Her attitude and demeanour spoke of something lying just underneath the surface, some sort of pain that Kyle wanted to tap into. If he could just get her to talk to him, perhaps he could score.

"You know, when I want to be alone, I don't really want to be alone. I just say I do. That way people will continue to bother me until I cheer up. It's funny how that works." Kyle was grasping at straws by this point.

Gritting her teeth, the next words came out like chewed gravel. "If I tell you what's the matter, will you leave me alone?"

"Absolutely." It was an in and Kyle was willing to exploit it.

"My boyfriend dumped me tonight of all nights. Fucking Valentine's Day and he dumps me. Me! Can you believe it?" The pain of the rejection was clearly written all over her face and permeated her words.

"Aww, Sweets, that's terrible! What a douchebag!"

"He is a douchebag..." and for the first time that night, she smiled, her face lighting up through the tears that fell.

"Let me buy you that drink, I swear it will get better." Kyle turned on the charm as he asked the question, hoping that she would agree.

Pausing for a moment before answering, she assessed him. "Sure, I'll have a Margarita."

"Excellent, I love the taste of limes!" A little over exuberant, Kyle wondered if perhaps she would figure out his intent.

"Me too! My name's Anna, by the way." Her rushed response gave no indication that she thought the comment was a little off.

Throughout the night, Kyle and Anna talked and laughed, each of them happy for the company. At the end of the night, Anna asked Kyle to walk her to her apartment. It was late and she was a little more than tipsy. To be perfectly honest, Kyle didn't mind. He was hoping to get a little before leaving her to sleep off her hangover. In the morning, she'd probably not remember much of the night or Kyle for that matter, chalking up the disorientation and dizziness to her alcohol consumption the night before. It was a perfect plan.

Once at the door to her building, Anna turned to him, her tequila infused breath warm across his face. "I know what you are."

"Oh yeah? What's that?" Kyle was surprised that she was being so bold. Most people didn't have the nerve to call a vampire by its name in this day and age.

"You're a nice guy," she answered, teetering on the impossibly high heels she wore. "Wanna kiss me?"

Leaning in, Kyle took what she offered so willingly. Anna clung to him as the kiss continued, her legs getting weak and her mind emptying of thought. Turning her neck to the side, she offered him a new area to kiss.

Kyle hesitated for a moment, pulling back to gaze into her face. Her eyes were serious and from the look of her, she had sobered up slightly during the kiss. Her head was still tilted to the side, an invitation to what she knew Kyle truly was.

Nestling his mouth over her jugular, he extended his fangs and sank them into her willing flesh, sucking up the sweet nectar of her blood..

Then Anna uttered the four words no vampire ever wants to hear…

"Are they in yet?"

JULIANNE SNOW

AN EXCERPT FROM

DAYS WITH THE UNDEAD: BOOK ONE

DAY 7

We moved fairly quickly through the countryside today. I don't like being out in the open for too long or too often because our movements tend to attract the unwanted attention of any of the Undead lurking around. Moving through the woods does have its drawbacks as well, but the dense underbrush acts as a warning system of sorts. The Undead don't have the foresight to move covertly by sticking to the trails. Their progress can be easily tracked and therefore avoided.

There was one moment where we thought that perhaps we would be stopped entirely. As we were going from one wooded area to the next, we had to cross a back road. The forest was dense on both sides of the road and we assumed that we would be able to walk the kilometer between them without any incident. What we didn't bank on was the officer that had chosen to set his speed trap on this desolate road in the middle of nowhere.

We stepped out of the woods just to the left of where he had tucked his cruiser behind a thick copse of trees. You have to imagine the sight that he saw; four people stepping out the woods decked out to the nines with weapons and other gear.

Within mere moments, the lights and sirens started, scaring the shit out of us. It was a sound that we hadn't heard in such a long time. In fact, it was a sound that we felt that we should have been hearing more of. It was an odd thing; we knew that most people are ineffectual against the Undead but we wanted that response from law enforcement, if only to feel that something was being done.

He sped the short distance to where we were stopped, not sure if we should just make a run for it or reassure him by waiting. He got out of the cruiser and immediately drew his service revolver. Considering that none of us had our firearms at the ready, it seemed like overkill in the moment. His questions came fast and somewhat garbled; we must have surprised him as much as he did us.

Not quite sure what to tell him, the truth came out instead. The look of disbelief that took hold of his countenance began to make us somewhat fearful. The last thing that we wanted was to encounter someone from law enforcement intent on making an issue out of our flight. His hand holding the gun started to shake. It was obvious that he had heard something about what was happening in and around Toronto. It was clear, however, that he hadn't made up his mind on what to believe yet.

At that moment, his radio squawked to life. There was a disturbance in the next town over and they needed someone to respond. All of the other officers that had been dispatched could no longer be raised on their radios. He took one long look at us and got into his car to leave.

The last words he spoke as he pointed down the road to the south still haunt me: Don't go in that direction. When he pulled the car onto the road he headed north. The message from the officer was clear; they're close.

Our aim was to get to a place where crossing into the United States would be easy. After losing Barbara, we needed to re-evaluate so we planned on paying someone, a local, to take us across. If all else failed, we were just going to 'borrow' a boat and navigate the waters ourselves.

Max and I had taken watercraft and boating lessons for this contingency but we couldn't be sure of the strength of the waters we might encounter. We hadn't come all of this way just to fail now. Being separated from the infection by water, I feel like I can breathe, at least for the moment anyways. This, though, is the terror we experienced in the last few moments of our lives in Canada.

We chose to cross into the United States by traversing the Saint Clair River. While most of both sides of the shore are industrialized, there are sections where the urbanization hasn't been improved as of yet. We picked one of those spots, hoping to remain unnoticed.

The shore was muddy, the dock rudimentary by comparison to those further upstream, and in the twilight you couldn't even see the opposite bank. There was no one to pay to take us across so we found a boat just large enough to safely hold us along with our gear. We choose something just big enough to handle and give us the peace of mind that we would not capsize. If our aim was true, once across we would be north of Detroit and hopefully have cut ourselves off from the Undead by major bodies of water.

There are, of course, the areas where the border is only just a figurative line. Places where no one guards the entrance into the United States. The places where no one monitors the exit out of Canada.

In the past, the relationship between Canada and the United States has been one of respect and helpfulness to a certain degree. The world's longest unprotected border does lie between us after all. Sure, there are border crossings with border guards on both sides but at times that's just a formality.

That was of course before 9/11 - since then things have changed, but that is to be expected. None of that was going to stop us though; border guards or not, we were getting into the United States.

In all honesty we could be putting ourselves into more danger. With the way that air travel works, anyone can get anywhere within a matter of hours. Think of the ramifications that could have if even one infected person managed to get on a plane.

I remember back to 2001 when a passenger on an international flight caused a huge controversy because they started to exhibit symptoms similar to Ebola shortly after arriving. It turned out she didn't have it, but the communities she passed through were terrified. The implications of an infected person transitioning from alive to undead aboard a domestic or international flight is truly terrifying. All of those people would have no means for escape. Sure, it's possible that the Air Marshal could effectively take care of one or two but their mandate is to use lethal force only if no other alternative is available. The confusion in that moment would be high. Would they make the right choice between restraint and death? Firing a gun aboard a plane during flight could be disastrous. What if they missed? What if things escalated and the pilot landed the plane? That could potentially unleash the infection into areas that hadn't been exposed to it yet. Horrifying to think about, but I digress from the topic at hand...

As soon as Max started the craft's engine, a noise came out of the woods to our backs. As I hurried to release the moorings, I ordered Ben and Bob to get the rest of our gear and themselves into the boat as soon as possible. I remember thinking, feeling almost intuitively that we didn't have time to waste.

Somehow I knew that noise was being made by them.

The noise we were hearing is hard to explain. It was like the sound of a stampede of cattle, only softer, more ominous. Ominous only because we know that only a significant number of the Undead would be able to make that much noise. The sound waves pushed at us, allowing us to feel their approach. If this is what it felt like to be on the front line during wars fought on the battlefields of old, I now understand what it must have felt like to stare down your enemy as it marched forward. You knew they were coming.

Then the smell hit us. I work with the dead so I'm almost immune to the smell of decomposition in the sense that I can readily recognize it and then ignore it. There was no ignoring this. We had never smelled them like this before.

The cloying scent of decomposition was overpowering. It was mixed with the smells of blood and dirt and what was almost sweat-like in odor but I think that's impossible. How can something dead sweat? The heat of the past few days certainly hadn't done anything to help with the stench and in the soft breeze of the evening, it robbed the breath from you.

I could hear my team behind me trying not to gag but failing as I unfastened the last of the lines securing the boat to the dock. At that moment they burst through the last of the trees along the edge of the shore. There were now at least a hundred or so of the Undead only a few arm lengths away.

The shock of that moment was unparalleled in anything that I can recently remember. There were so many of them. I gave the boat a hard shove away from the dock and jumped aboard. Max opened the throttle as the Undead poured from the woods like honey from a broken bottle, their arms reaching for us. They were so close that you could feel the wind from their hands as they just missed you. The boat surged forward, throwing us off balance. How we managed to remain in the boat during the panic of that moment is beyond me.

In their haste and desire to follow us, some fell into the water but their bloated bodies just bobbed on the surface slowly before sinking. I hate to imagine that they are walking to the opposite shore underneath the water as I type this - that they will meet us here.

Without the benefit of their senses (if they have any), I hope they are lost forever, that the currents take them far away to the bottom of Lake St. Clair or further along to Lake Erie. Actually, I don't wish that. I don't want them contaminating the water supply. There are water treatment plants along the shores and that could be even more disastrous if this situation is somehow brought under control. And we certainly don't want to think of them as fish bait. I don't know if the organism, if it is in fact an organism, has the capability to jump species and I would rather not find out.

Once we were on open water, we felt safer. Our journey to the opposite shore was rather uneventful after the earlier tense, terrifying moments. We did lose some of our supplies but they were non-essential so we're not too bad off. We can restock. The important thing is that we are all still alive.

I hope everyone reading this out there is safe. Please pray for us on our journey. I don't want to get too hopeful in thinking that we may have gotten in front of the infection but we will be moving further south.

Godspeed to anyone else out there in a similar struggle.

DAY 8

Moving through the United States is a little more difficult. Four individuals moving quickly on foot, armed to the hilt tends to attract some attention.

In Canada, no one bothered with us. Must have been part of the Canadian way of life; natural curiosity is rampant but along with that is a healthy respect for privacy. Then, of course, you factor in the Undead component and it becomes a completely different ball game. No one bothers you, and you don't bother anyone else.

Our guess was that people in the United States felt a kind of safety in the fact that they live in the glorious United States of America, Land of the Free. I hate to break it to you but the Undead aren't going to stop at the border. Your military is not going be able to keep all of you safe especially since they haven't even appeared to mobilize yet.

There's nothing on the internet, no inkling of any increased presence despite the tip that there has been a possible outbreak in upstate New York. The major news website has little information coming out of the area and their crew on the scene has gone missing. The situation does not bode well at the moment and if you're reading this and you are anywhere near that town, anywhere in upstate New York or even in New York State at all, I would suggest leaving immediately.

It's only going to spread farther and farther. That's obvious by what's already happened. The Undead managed to get all the way to the St. Clair River and that's not an easy feat. It took us just over six days to get there ourselves and we were moving with a purpose.

There is a sense of relief to be out of Canada, mind you. There is so much more space and options for travel in the United States. Where we were in Canada, it would have been hard to get around the Great Lakes if we found that we couldn't get into the United States. We had unknowingly funneled ourselves into a do or die situation. We had no option other than to get out.

I know that leaving is hard. But you have to make the choice to survive or die trying. The more of us left to fight the growing tide, the better. I know that many of you don't know how to fight or what you're fighting exactly but it has come to the point that none of us can sit idly by and just let them take it all from us.

My group has given me permission to tell you their stories, to tell you why and how they got here. I'm not going to give it to you all at once though. Each one of us has a story that deserves to be told, and the time to tell it will present itself accordingly.

Given the situation and how hard I know it is for you all to make that choice to leave, I'm going to tell you about Max today. If this doesn't convince you to get up and move south, there is no hope for you...

Max served in the Canadian Military from the time that he was old enough to enlist. He was never what you would call book smart, but he had the intelligence of a strategist and it served him well in Afghanistan. His skill with firearms made him a natural choice to be trained as a sniper. On assignment he was able to filter through the information he was being fed and assess the situation as it unfolded in front of him.

There were times that he went against orders but it always turned out that he made the correct choice. Most men would have been court-marshaled for such a disregard of the chain of command, but even his superiors began to trust his instincts in the field. It didn't allow him to rise through the ranks, but he was happy to know that the lives he took had little collateral damage.

Shortly after enlisting he married his high school sweetheart Melinda. The two were the perfect pair in public - always kind and loving to each other. Many of the other military wives looked to Max and wondered why their husbands couldn't be more like him. He did anything for Melinda and vice versa. They wanted badly to start a family and while they tried to have children it just wasn't in the cards for them. After repeated tests and specialists, it was determined that both of them were less than fertile.

It was a huge blow to the two of them but it seemed to affect Melinda more. Even though they both had a measure of responsibility, Melinda squarely took the blame upon herself. She spiraled into depression and there was nothing that Max could do to snap her out of it. With Max still on the active duty roister, they couldn't adopt. It made getting out an important step for Max. He just wanted her to be happy. To smile again.

So he put in for early retirement and when it came through, December 23rd was Max's last day overseas. He was coming home to spend Christmas with his wife after his final tour. He was excited to be able to spend time with her and to start the adoption process in the New Year. This time that would be spent between them was much needed as he had felt the strain that serving in the military had put on their relationship.

He was somewhere over the Atlantic when the accident occurred.

Melinda had been out at the mall finishing her Christmas shopping. As she was walking to her car through the parking lot, she was struck by an SUV. The Sport Utility Vehicle choose to flee the scene and as a result Melinda wasn't found until another shopper noticed her crumpled body where it had landed between two parked cars, shopping bags still clenched tightly in her fists. While she survived, she never regained consciousness.

Max was told of the accident the moment that he landed. He was devastated. After he landed, he did nothing but sit next to her bedside and pray that she would return to him. It was very sad to go and visit Melinda, to witness what her condition was doing to him.

The accident with Melinda hit us all hard. Steve, my husband, was her brother and I had always regarded Melinda as the sister I never had. It was heartbreaking to watch as the days turned to weeks, then months. We tried to remain optimistic but we all knew that hope was waning. It was even more difficult to understand and cope with because the police had no leads on who had done this to her.

Max moved Melinda home on May 15th and hired in-home care to look after all of her needs. The hope was that familiar surroundings might trigger something, helping her to break out of her own mind. It was a horrible time for the whole family. None of us really knew what to do or what to say to him. All we could do was pray and hope for the best.

Then came May 29th. That just might have been the hardest day of Max's life. He knew that he couldn't take her with him in her current condition. It was going to be rough enough for the rest of us on foot. Melinda needed the constant flow of oxygen from the ventilator in order to survive. But he also knew that if he left her like she was, it was only a matter of time before the Undead found her. And that thought chilled him to the bone.

We waited while Max made his decision; saw him agonizing over it for hours. Long hours while the city filled with the Undead. You could feel him willing her to wake up but we all knew that wasn't going to happen.

In the end, he decided that the best course of action was to let her die peacefully by disconnecting her ventilator. He would then keep vigil on the chance that she returned. No one thought that would be the case, as she hadn't come into contact with anyone infected but we just didn't know for sure. It was something he did alone, choosing to say his final goodbye in private.

Our only answer to his vigil over her body was the single retort from his gun and the gut wrenching sobs from the other end of the house.

Within minutes he was out, composed and shatteringly vacant. Then we were gone. The moment not forgotten but strangely beyond us at this point.

A few days ago, Max quietly told me that he hadn't waited for Melinda to die. He said that he couldn't bear watching her body struggle as it asphyxiated. We had all assumed that she had come back, had become one of the Undead, but that wasn't the case. And I'm not surprised that he shared his secret with me. I know the pain he had felt in that moment. Shooting someone you love is... difficult.

So please do not wait until it's too late. Give yourself the chance to survive.

DAY 9

Making our way further south has been fairly easy the past day or so. Keeping ahead of the Undead has been easy as well. I don't think we've even seen one since crossing the channel between Lake Huron and Lake St. Clair. Despite our lack of seeing the Undead, we know they are behind us, slowly making their way in their never-ending parody of a putrefied parade.

We've managed to make good time, skirting around the highly urban areas in Michigan State; trying to evade as much notice as possible. We are finally starting to see some movement of people but it's nothing like what we witnessed coming out of Toronto and the surrounding suburbs.

We've been talking a lot about the mass exodus of Toronto in the past twelve hours. Talking about how we haven't seen hardly a soul make it as far as we have. Wondering what route others may have taken. Then it occurs to you, did some just stop, thinking that they had gone far enough? Did others just give up moving forward and allow themselves to be absorbed into the masses of the Undead?

It's heart wrenching to think that people could just lie down to accept a fate worse than death like that but in the face of something so pervasively evil who could blame them?

We decided we should attempt to make better time. There was just no way that we were going to get through the continental United States without some form of transportation, so we 'borrowed' a 4×4 truck from a long-term parking facility and hoped it would help get us as far south as possible. We figured that travelling in the truck would make us less conspicuous and a lot more protected against the Undead and the possibility of piracy.

It also gave us the huge advantage of moving at night, something we'd been unable to do on foot, so long as the roads remained clear ahead of us. Did I mention we might even be able to sleep a little more soundly? Sleep was something in short supply with us and being able to sleep two at a time in a protected space was like giving candy to a bunch of kids. It was like we'd won the lottery.

We were trying to figure out who would get the first sleep shift when Ben noticed something odd off to the west in a field next to the road. A few sheep were acting strangely and pressing themselves so forcefully up against their fencing that it looked like they were going to break through it.

Bob pulled the truck over as both Ben and I got out our binoculars and focused in on the sheep, noting the heavy breathing and panicked looks on their normally vacant faces. Movement caught my eye just to the left and I noticed that the rest of the field appeared to be littered with gory carcasses.

My first thought was of a predator like a coyote but the longer I stared the more my mind began to focus on the real culprit. My blood ran cold as I reached out and touched Ben's arm. His only words were "My God..." The last few sheep were gone in mere minutes, consumed by the voracious appetites of the swarm of chipmunks.

Undead fucking chipmunks.

Forget the cute little furry friends you talk to in your backyard; these were die-hard, eat the flesh right off your bones critters. Once done with the sheep, the swarming mass of them started to head in our direction.

Bob put the car back into gear as Max and I made sure that all the vents and windows in the truck were closed tightly. The swarm moved quickly, much faster than any 'human' Undead we'd ever seen. They broke out onto the road behind us keeping a fairly good pace, Bob only being able to go so fast on the broken dirt road. Up ahead we could see a stop sign, a level meeting of two roads and we could see for a few kilometers in each direction. It was a safe bet that we would be able to run the stop sign and not risk being overrun by them.

In the distance coming from the west I noticed a yellow school bus approaching the intersection. Focusing through my binoculars I could see the open windows with the small hands hanging out to feel the wind. See the innocent, joyful faces of the children probably on their way home from school.

Hastily judging speed and distance, it was obvious that the bus was going to get to the intersection prior to our truck. Looking behind us I could see that the swarm was gaining ground on us with each passing moment.

We had a decision to make: blow through the stop sign and hope for the best, sacrificing those innocent kids to the horde, or slow down and let the mass of rodents overtake us, hoping that the school bus was not going to turn in our direction at the intersection.

There really was no discussion.

We all knew what we had to do.

While we all wanted to survive, to outlast the infection, we knew that we could not sacrifice a bus load of innocent children to do so. We had the means to possibly fight our way out of an encounter with the Undead chipmunks, but we knew that those children did not.

Our collective mind made up, Bob started to slow the truck down by applying the brake. Through the back window I could see the ravenous horde getting closer. It was a stunningly terrifying sight to see the solid, teeming mass of bloodied fur almost float toward us.

And then, we were still, the car having come to a complete stop.

We all unsheathed our hunting knives, getting ready for the moment that we would have to fight. Knowing in our minds that one bite would be enough to infect us.

Enough to turn one of us into one of them.

Within a few seconds, we could hear the sounds of tiny nails on the car, not unlike the sound of nails on a chalkboard. It started to get darker in the car as the swarm covered us. Through the windows you could see their little undead faces pressed up hard against the glass. Their beady little white eyes boring into you. It was truly terrifying, those moments where we stared into the faces of hell.

And then as quickly as they were upon us, they moved on. Bob had left the motor running on the truck effectively sealing off most of the engine cavity from them. That was probably what saved us, to be perfectly honest.

Or perhaps it was the fact that the bus had stopped just to the east of the intersection in order to let a little girl with blonde pigtails disembark.

The horde in its entirety was now moving toward that school bus and that little girl. All we could do was watch in absolute horror as the young girl noticed the swarm coming toward her. For a moment she was still, but then she realized what was coming at her was not a good thing. We watched those little pigtails flying out behind her as her too-big backpack shifted on her back as she ran. Ran for her young life.

The mass of undead chipmunks split. Some chased the girl, and the others aimed for the bus loaded with prey. The young girl was knocked down by the force of them climbing on her small frame; her terrified screams a warning signal to the driver of the bus who stopped to see what had happened.

Each of us willed the bus to start moving again but we knew that they were all going to die; the bus with all of its open windows became a feeding ground for them. The sound was terrible, heartbreaking, and sickening. Not wanting to watch any further, Bob accelerated hard and blew through the intersection.

We just drove. Further and further away. The sounds of the day relentlessly haunting us.

We had no idea that the infection could jump species. It was something that we had never even considered. How do you protect yourself against an Undead animal world? The discovery terrified us to the core of our very beings.

The game definitely changed at that point. It's time for everyone to wake up and get moving before it's too late. There will be no sleep for us again tonight. Not with this hanging over our heads.

Please pray for survival…

ABOUT THE AUTHOR

Julianne Snow is the author of the *Days with the Undead* series and the founder of Zombieholics Anonymous. She writes within the realms of speculative fiction, has roots that go deep into horror and is a member of the Horror Writers Association. Julianne has pieces of short fiction in publications from Sirens Call Publications, Open Casket Press, 7DS Books, James Ward Kirk Publishing, Coffin Hop Press and Hazardous Press with many shorts to be released soon.

Social Media Links

Twitter: @CdnZmbiRytr

Facebook: Julianne Snow

FB Fan Page: Julianne Snow, Author

Blogs: Days with the Undead & The FlipSide of Julianne

Zombieholics Anonymous can be found on Facebook, Twitter and zombieholicsanonymous.com

31809027R00076

Made in the USA
Charleston, SC
29 July 2014